Metaphorosis

July 2019

Beautifully made speculative fiction

Also from Metaphorosis Books

Score – an SFF symphony

Reading 5X5: Readers' Edition
Reading 5X5: Writers' Edition

Best Vegan Science Fiction & Fantasy

Best Vegan SFF of 2018
Best Vegan SFF of 2017
Best Vegan SFF of 2016

Metaphorosis Magazine

Metaphorosis: Best of 2018
Metaphorosis: Best of 2017
Metaphorosis: Best of 2016

Metaphorosis 2018: The Complete Stories
Metaphorosis 2017: The Complete Stories
Metaphorosis 2016: Nearly Complete Stories

Monthly issues

by B. Morris Allen

Susurrus
Allenthology: Volume I
Tocsin: and other stories
Start with Stones: collected stories
Metaphorosis: a collection of stories

Metaphorosis

July 2019

edited by
B. Morris Allen

Metaphorosis Books

Neskowin

ISSN: 2573-136X (online)
ISBN: 978-1-64076-143-8 (e-book)
ISBN: 978-1-64076-144-5 (paperback)

July 2019

One Day in Space Too Many

Michael Sherrin

Day 1: Gerry woke to his chiming alarm clock, unaware his spaceship, the *Rotor*, had just exploded. He shuffled into the kitchen and expected his usual routine: frying eggs, watering his bonsai, and being the only person for light-years.

But there he was, already holding the frying pan.

Gerry rubbed his eyes, wondering if he had actually woken up. "You're…" he said.

"Me?" said his mirror image, staring back with the same bewilderment. They pointed at each other, silent, mouths open. The other dropped the pan and shook his fingers.

Gerry stumbled backward. He wondered just how vivid a dream could be.

Loneliness had been his way of life, but that might be reaching its limits. It had been three months since he'd been in a room with another person, though he wasn't sure if seeing himself counted. It seemed best to identify the cause of this hallucination before taking drastic action.

Then, he noticed a plant on the counter and spun back to his cabin. His own bonsai, Rita, was still on his nightstand. Feeling his chest tighten, he sat on the bed, wondering if his copy remained outside. He touched the soil, but didn't feel what he expected.

"Rita needs some water," Gerry said, carrying the bonsai to the kitchen.

The copy took a cup from the shelf and slotted it under the sink without taking his eyes off the little tree. He passed the filled cup across the counter.

Gerry poured the water over the soil as he had the day before. "You should check yours."

The other Gerry checked his bonsai's soil, then filled another cup without speaking.

Gerry worried his hallucination theory was breaking down. Watching himself was unnerving yet familiar. He backed up to the computer terminal and tapped the screen to confirm his suspicion. "Shit."

"What?" the other Gerry asked.

"The log is exactly the same as yesterday," he said, partly to himself. "Sensor, radiation levels, stellar cartography. Even the date is the same."

Today, it seemed, was yesterday.

Gerry slumped into a chair and rubbed his forehead. "My memory's fuzzy. Something triggered an alarm, I think."

"Will it happen again?"

These cargo ships were completely automated. The company was supposed to assign two crew for unexpected occurrences, but they got by with one and pocketed the profits. Gerry liked it that way – just him, his bonsai, and uninterrupted quiet. It would be another four months until delivery. He wasn't sure if he could tolerate that time with another person, especially himself.

This wasn't a hallucination. Whatever had caused it, he needed to reverse it.

He switched between consoles, examining every variable he could think of. His doppelganger sat to the side, leaping up when an alert sounded.

"Gravitational waves increasing," Gerry said. "This area is affecting our warp drive."

"Where's it coming from?"

"I'm not reading a source of mass."

Gerry tapped buttons on the console.

"You're overloading the warp drive?" Other Gerry asked.

Co-pilots wanted to discuss plans of action, but Gerry preferred to act. "If we survive and it happens again, then I'll change variable by variable." The 'we' was hard to say.

It took an hour to reconfigure the drive. His doppelganger knew everything he knew, yet it was impossible to work together. Every time he moved to a console, the other Gerry was there in his way. Space was supposed to be empty.

Once the drive was reconfigured, Gerry buckled into his seat, with his copy next to him.

He opened his console, squeezed his eyes shut, and pressed enter.

The *Rotor* exploded with two crew members aboard.

Gerry woke to his alarm chiming. He waved it off and hurried into the kitchen.

Other Gerry held the pan in his hand.

The control room doors opened and a new Gerry walked in, holding his bonsai. "Any better ideas?"

This time, Gerry reversed the engines.

The *Rotor* exploded, three crew members aboard.

Gerry woke and ran into the kitchen, his alarm still chiming.

One Gerry dropped the pan of eggs. Another entered from the control room. A third sat on the couch with his bonsai on the table.

Gerry tried turning the ship.

The *Rotor* exploded, four crew members aboard.

He shut down all non-essential systems.

The *Rotor* exploded, five crew members aboard.

He shut down all systems.

The *Rotor* exploded, six crew members aboard.

Loop 65: The ship carried enough food and supplies for an entire planet, and the

cargo returned each loop, so they all helped themselves to anything they liked. Space was the limited resource. Gerry 2 directed the population to the cargo bay as the living quarters was becoming overcrowded.

Loop 71: Several Gerrys formed a team to study the phenomenon trapping them. They reviewed data from the ship's database, scanned stories of past phenomena, and examined the ship's functions. They sent out a distress call, but doubted it would reach anyone.

Loop 73: When Gerry walked down the corridor, everyone stood aside, as they would for a captain. Some even saluted, something he hadn't seen since his military days. It made him feel like escape was all his responsibility. He avoided the cargo bay and spent most of his time in his cabin.

Loop 92: Gerry 5 believed he'd found the reason for the loops. "The ship has a failsafe in case of a catastrophic failure. It's like a saved state made of a bend in space-time that returns to the last safe position. It's only supposed to work on inanimate substances."

"Protect the cargo at any cost," Gerry said, recalling the first rule in the company handbook. "Can we revert to an earlier save?" He had started coming to the science meetings at Gerry 2's urging.

"No. It can only store one save. Even if we could turn it off, which we can't, we'd all die in the next explosion."

Escape had many meanings, Gerry thought.

"This area of space is creating a feedback of negative energy, which is conflicting with the drive. The save state isn't just resetting space and matter; we're actually traveling back to that point in time, all of us. It's like we're wrapping a piece of string around our finger, and with each loop, we add another layer of string."

Loop 104: While Gerry 58 was attempting to bypass the quantum energy distributor, a valve exploded and killed him. His body was found burned, but it disappeared at the start of the next loop.

Loop 105: "You need to say something," Gerry 2 said. "No one thought we could die."

Gerry focused on bending wire around Rita's branches, exerting just enough force to guide them into position without damaging the structure. The wiring reset each loop, which gave him reason to spend hours in his cabin repeating the process, away from his copies and clones.

There was a reason he liked flying alone, but that reality had been crushed under spatial anomalies. This was the first death on the ship. It was like getting sad over a broken branch, one offshoot of little importance to the overall growth.

He almost believed that.

Loop 186: An attempt at using antimatter to stabilize the warp drive caused an explosion that killed ten Gerrys. All systems were back to working order the next loop.

Loop 219: The science team suggested using the lifeboat to send one person out for rescue. Gerry 98 volunteered. The entire ship watched the lifeboat float until it disappeared into the blackness.

Loop 220: Gerry 98 re-appeared on the ship. Gerry 220 started that morning in the docked lifeboat.

Loop 357: A fight broke out over use of a video console. This wasn't the first fight, but it was the first Gerry on Gerry death.

"This could get worse," Gerry 2 said.

"What should I do about it?" Gerry asked.

"You're the original."

"I never listened to a chain of command before, why should I start now?"

Loop 422: Fights became more commonplace as space became more constrained. New Gerrys began loops atop cargo pods and in service tubes, places where their predecessors had gone for privacy. Every corner of the ship had become a makeshift restroom.

Loop 435: Gerry 2 organized gardening sessions to manage the forest of bonsais sprouting along the bulkheads. There was an understood comradery between a Gerry and his tree. It was the one thing each of them owned. But not everyone was willing to put the time in. Some trees were cultivated and managed, while others grew large and unkempt. Gerry 2 hoped gardening would relax the building tension. He also hoped Gerry would join in.

Loop 453: Every morning, the Gerrys expelled most of the cargo pods to make room for themselves. Gerry 361 set up a soccer tournament using a ball they'd found, though all the scores had to be memorized because anything written down would disappear.

Loop 459: Gerry had no interest in the games or community gardening. It had been more than a year, yet he saw a different person on each duplicate's face. All his routines had ended – no more cooking, no more jogging up and down the ship, no quiet time to read or rest. There were more than 400 others to contend with.

Loop 730: Gerry 2 planned a party for the two-year anniversary on the ship. Gerry 467 and Gerry 544 fought over one of the few beers available. Gerry 544 broke Gerry 467's nose.

Loop 758: There was a disagreement over the team standings in the league. Everyone remembered something different. They debated until punches flew. Some Gerrys fled to the control room and sealed the door.

The fighting continued through the next loop, with Gerrys running from their starting position to the battle.

Loop 761: The fighting subsided. At least 100 Gerrys had died.

Loop 762: Gerry walked through the clean cargo bay, devoid of any signs of fighting except for the reduced numbers. It was a struggle to comprehend, like part of him had fought another part and neither side had won. This was a different kind of self-hatred.

But this wasn't the military. There were no court marshals or tribunals to convene, no punishments to enact. How could he blame anyone for what had happened? Wasn't he as guilty as they were?

No one spoke. Everyone stopped moving and watched him.

"Just because the cargo bay is clean, it doesn't mean you are," Gerry said. "If you can't handle being here, there's an airlock for each of you."

There was nothing that could stop more fighting. They were only going to get more cramped, more strained, and more angry.

Loop 1,370: Gerry 5, the head of the science team, died during a riot. Gerry disbanded the science team.

Gerry 2 argued against giving up, but Gerry no longer believed in escape.

He wondered what was happening outside the loop. Had time continued moving? Had someone come looking? He had no family to worry about him, but a ship full of cargo was an expensive thing to lose. He liked to think that meant someone cared.

Loop 1,723: The airlock to the cargo bay was opened minutes after the loop started. Several hundred Gerrys and their bonsais were jettisoned into space. No one saw who did it.

Loop: 2,184: Gerry 2 hurt his leg carrying boxes to the kitchen. Gerry let him stay in the cabin to recover.

Loop 2,508: The Second Gerry War began over accusations of a stolen bonsai.

Loop 2,513: The Second Gerry War ended. The bonsai in question was crushed in the fighting.

Loop 4,147: While handing out lunch in the cargo bay, Gerry 2 got caught in the crossfire of punches and was knocked against a bulkhead. He died the next loop.

Gerry secluded himself in his cabin.

Loop 4,150: Gerry emerged and reformed the science team. He had developed a system for oral record keeping so no single person contained all the research. There were dozens of volunteers to join, and the petty fighting subsided for a while.

Loop 4,682: Gerry 127 tried opening the cargo bay doors again, but was caught in the act.

Gerry had to decide what to do. Hundreds had died the last time, and the numbers would have been much larger this loop.

Gerry sat on the bed in his cabin and stared at the alarm clock. It chimed every morning, though he never set it. Every morning started the same way. For almost twelve years, he had woken to see Gerry 2 making eggs, but that didn't happen anymore. The routine had ended.

He expelled Gerry 127 into space.

Loop 5,731: The Sixth Gerry War ended with more than a thousand casualties.

Loop 6,574: Forty-three Gerrys died of cancer over the years. Several committed suicide. Counts were difficult as bodies often disappeared before discovery.

Loop 7,758: Gerry noticed his cabin door was ajar. He pressed the latch, and someone lunged at him with a butcher's knife. He slid backward, bending out of reach. The assassin fell forward, then jumped up with impressive speed. Three other Gerrys rushed to restrain the assassin.

Gerry already had a limp from a failed attempt on his life years before. It had become a regular occurrence.

But there was a casualty. Dirt spread across the floor like a nebula, with Rita sprawled out, roots flat and broken, having been stomped to splinters by her assassin.

Loop 7,759: The loop cleaned Rita away.

There were no apologies or forgiveness. This was self-mutilation, a cruelty fostered by copies who couldn't adjust. Some wanted freedom by any means. Some thought an escape plan was being kept secret. Gerry was a figurehead by virtue of his age, not by skill. He'd learned this required a strict, unquestioning approach.

He expelled his attempted assassin into space. This was the eight time he done so.

Loop 8,152: The science team spent the past year collecting as much data on the explosion as possible. Gerry spent hours at the computer reviewing data and analysis, ignoring the aches and pains that came with his advanced age.

He finalized a simulation that recounted the explosion. It had to be recoded each loop, with each team member typing their assigned snippet into a console, and Gerry compiling them together. This led to the decisive discovery.

"The lifeboat," Gerry 80 said. "This time, it'll work."

Gerry leaned on his cane. He wore glasses, a pair he had to fish out from cargo every morning. His hair had gone completely gray. "The lifeboat only saves one."

"That's true."

Gerry frowned, then nodded for Gerry 80 to continue.

"Our ship is causing the loop. But the lifeboat doesn't generate a warp field. It can't fly at superluminal speeds, though a single passenger could survive several weeks with food and stasis."

Gerry rubbed his leg. "How would it work?"

Gerry 80 pointed to the screen. "It's like we have two doorways on opposite walls, but we go through one door and come out the other. Everything we've tried has been based on brute forcing our way through the doors, going faster and faster until we can break out of this negative space. But the balance is off – we can't break out until we have the same amount of positive energy here as there's negative energy out there."

Gerry watched the simulation play out. He had spent a third of his life on the *Rotor*, and it seemed hard to believe an end was in sight. This would only save one. There were thousands of Gerrys – thousands of himself onboard. He'd worked with them, talked with them, fought with them. What would happen when only one got free? "What do you need?"

"We need more of us."

Loop 11,753: Launch day. Calculations specified the amount of mass needed, the exact trajectory, and the precise timing to launch the lifeboat. After that, everything was unknown – escape, rescue, survival. Nothing was certain.

A few hundred Gerrys crammed onto the docking bay to watch. A video feed was setup in the cargo bay.

It had taken three years longer than estimated to reach this point. There had been too many deaths and not enough hope. Gerry had focused constant attention to keep the peace. He oversaw sport tournaments, held readings from his favorite books, and cultivated a group to care for the many orphaned bonsais. He was about eighty years old, his exact age impossible to count, yet he felt younger than ever. More active. More useful.

Standing at the edge of the dock, Gerry saw a timeline of himself aging backward down the corridor. It was as if time travel had penetrated the ship's hull and created a loop in that room. He saw himself smiling, scared, frustrated, and jealous. Each held their bonsai, a forest of twisting branches and gnarled roots, some in bloom, some pure green, and a few browned and frayed yet clutched with the same pride. These copies had once been nothing but offshoots he could neither control nor prune. He had as much relation to the newest versions as a great-grandfather had with his descendants. They had their own experiences, memories, and lives on this ship.

They were all him. The best and worst on display.

He rubbed his eyes under his glasses, brushing tears aside. He had the privilege of watching himself survive. It was reassuring to think at least part of him could begin anew.

A random Gerry had been selected from the computer. 10,377. They had limited the selection list to Gerrys between one to five years old – someone young, but experienced enough to explain what had happened should they find someone to tell.

Gerry 10,377 opened the door to the lifeboat and slid inside, holding his bonsai on his lap.

Gerry began the countdown, and every Gerry on the ship called out numbers in unison. Five. Four. Three. Two. One. The lifeboat launched. It slid out from the ship, spun on its axes, and fell behind.

Soon, the gravitational forces would increase, the warp drive would strain under the pressure, and the ship would explode as it had thousands of times before. But this time, the force of that explosion would be enough to propel the lifeboat across the horizon and into normal space.

Gerry couldn't answer what would happen on the ship. Would the loops continue or would this break the cycle? Escape might become a daily occurrence. The idea made him smile.

He pressed his palm against the airlock window. It was reassuring to be with the rest of himself aboard the ship.

The starship freighter *Rotor* exploded with 6,322 crew members aboard.

Day 2: Gerry woke up in the lifeboat, alone.

See Michael Sherrin's story "One Day in Space Too Many" online at Metaphorosis.
If you liked it, leave a comment. Authors love that!
Remember to subscribe to our e-mail updates so you'll know when new stories are posted.

About the story

I've found a lot of inspiration from books on cosmology and physics. This story came after reading "Time Travel in Einstein's Universe" by J. Richard Gott, where he explained how a Groundhog Day-like time loop might occur. He showed this phenomenon would actually duplicate the person looping, and this stuck with me as a fascinating twist on the oft-repeated formula.

The rest of the story evolved organically where one person would have to deal with thousands of copies of themself over an extended period of time. The intention wasn't to ground the narrative in hard science, but rather to explore the science of such a time loop. That is, how would an individual deal with having his space and self invaded in such an extreme way? Thus, Gerry exists alone on a large ship that can conveniently accommodate thousands of people, but all he wants is to be alone.

A question for the author

Q: What do you think is the single most important quality for a good writer to possess?

A: I think the single most important quality for a good writer is curiosity. Curiosity, whether it's in history, science, psychology, or some other arena, leads to fresh ideas that can be become a captivating story. Being curious compels the writer to ask more questions: Why does this happen? How does this work? What would it be like if viewed through a different lens? When a writer considers the possible answers to these questions, they are poised to develop interesting characters in believable, well-established settings. There are many traits needed to succeed in the fundamentals of writing, including patience, perseverance, tolerance for criticism, and commitment. However, it's curiosity that makes writing fun.

About the author

Michael Sherrin developed his preference for fiction when he learned reality didn't include a real Spider-Man. He has an MBA from the Kellogg School of Management, where he learned to write riveting Excel formulas, though the solutions were often predictable. By day, he works with complex analytical algorithms, and by night he works on short stories and his novel.

Michael lives outside Boston with his husband, dog, and several thousand action figures.

www.prodigeek.com, @prodigeek

A Layer Thin As Breath

Thea Boodhoo

"Valley. Can you still hear me?"

Julian's voice filtered through her dying radio. The *Prince of Cats* was a speck of light, dimming through the gold-grey film that, atom by atom, was devouring her helmet.

Valley tried to say something, anything. Failed.

Julian was sobbing on the other end. "I'm so sorry. I'm so, so kzzzzzzchchchcffft —" and that was it. Her radio was gone.

"Oh god," she breathed to herself, to no one. "Oh god," *I don't want to die. I don't want to die.* She sobbed once, twice, and then, with tears pooling in her eyes and the *Prince of Cats* invisible through the liquid, she found a pocket of calm, like stepping from a noisy bar onto a cool, quiet street.

Something brushed against her hand, and she cried out, startled. Her vision was still blurred by tears, and the thing dissolving her space suit was like an iridescent veil across the glass of her helmet, but through it all she could see the outline of her hand.

Not her glove.

Her hand.

The veil, delicate as a cobweb when it had floated innocuously through space, was finally at the layer of her skin. It felt like cool air at first, then like nothing. Then her fingernails tickled.

She was so surprised to see her bare hand, covered only in iridescent gauze, against the black of space, without the sensation of it freezing solid, that she forgot she was dying.

When she remembered, she screamed again. And as she screamed, the iridescent veil dissolved the final layer of her helmet glass and fell toward her face.

Hyperventilating, she felt it against her nose and forehead, cheeks and lips, like cold mist, and every time her breath sucked in, the thing moved further into her mouth. She tried to spit it out, but in it came, in and in and in, forcing past her coughing and gagging, pushing into her nose and ears, and–

And she could see again. It had absorbed her tears.

Her spacesuit was gone.

She was still alive.

Her scalp itched. She touched her head — her hair was gone, and her fingertips felt strangely sensitive, on the edge of pain. She looked at her hands — her fingernails were almost gone. The itching faded, and she felt the cobweb against every centimeter of her skin, enveloping her like water. It squeezed. It squeezed everywhere until she could barely breathe — and then released the moment before panic overtook her again.

It was in her eyes, but it didn't resist as she blinked.

Her eyelashes were gone.

It wrapped around her teeth and tongue, against the roof of her mouth and the inside of her cheeks. She tried to swallow, and felt it lining her esophagus.

Nausea overcame her. She dry heaved until the feeling faded.

She floated through space, holding her knees and crying tears that were immediately absorbed, breathing without drawing air into her lungs, the spidersilk feel of the space thing that enveloped her like impossibly thin gloves between the skin of her hands, which should be frozen, and her shins, which should also be frozen.

The cobweb had penetrated every part of her. It had eaten every strand of hair and every fingernail and toenail. She was left with nothing else, like a forgotten mannequin in a dusty storeroom.

She realized she was in shock. But she wasn't dead. She felt her toes and squeezed one where there should have been a toenail. It hurt.

Ok. It hurt. *Ok. I really am alive.*

Valley dreamed of all the ways this could have been avoided, tracing back the sequence of events all the way to her first fossil hunting trip with her parents when she was five. She cursed them for it. Then cried again. She put the memory away. *No. You've taken everything else, you can't have that.*

Valley had still been working on her PhD when she and Julian found the first fossil. It was a small mystery, like a crumpled piece of laundry with a too-regular microtexture, on a Kuiper Belt meteorite on Titan. When the press release came out, tech billionaire Linda Wallis convinced herself — or at least her board — that it was extraterrestrial technology. She'd recruited Valley and Julian, a crew, and the *Prince of Cats* to go looking for 'live ones' in the Kuiper Belt. It was a crazy long shot, like Jefferson sending Lewis and Clark after mastodons. The media went crazy when Linda announced she was going herself. Valley hadn't believed the technology hype, preferring the biological explanation she'd defended in her thesis. But the promise of exotic tech, and Linda's force of personality, won the expedition ample funding.

And they did find 'live ones'. Whether they were biological or technological seemed irrelevant after that. They seemed to feed on icy bodies, floating between Kuiper Belt objects like motes of dust in a dark room. Harmless, delicate, beautiful when the light caught them.

And now...

Something was crawling on her arm. It startled her out of her regrets. She grabbed at the spot that tickled, but found only cobweb. The feeling of the layers brushing against each other between her fingers and her forearm was firm and smooth, as if her skin were made of silk. It looked impossibly delicate — she could still see her brown skin through its iridescence — yet it was strong enough to keep her pressurized in the vacuum of space. The vibrations moved around her body, touching every part with varying strength before finally fading.

What is it doing? How am I alive?

It must be producing oxygen inside my respiratory system. She held her breath and counted. Thirty, sixty, a hundred and sixty... she didn't need to inhale. *OK that's not disconcerting at all.* She tried not to think about it, failed, started to panic again.

She was distracted by a light flickering across her shoulder. Then her arm.

At first she thought it was coming from a ship she couldn't see. She tried to look behind her, but without leverage it was impossible. As the glow steadily increased and moved across her body, she realized it was the cobweb making it, emitting light against every surface it touched. Just like the vibrations. *This is starting to feel like a calibration sequence.*

Wait. Was that it? Was it trying to communicate? Blindly trying every spectrum?

"Sound," she said. "I use sound! Talk to me!"

A vibration started in her throat, then moved out across her face and became a voice as it approached her ears. It was her own voice.

"Sound," it said. "I use sound! Talk to me!"

OK, space cobweb. This, I can do.

It might have been hours or millennia before they reached a planet. Valley's periods of unconsciousness were indeterminate, and each time she awoke, the stars were a mess. Constellations kept shifting, changing shape, and disappearing altogether. She didn't know enough astronomy to guess where the cobweb was taking her, but everything she knew about physics told her it was impossibly far. She assumed her periods of unconsciousness were long cryogenic sleeps — but how long? How much time had passed? Was anyone she knew still alive? Did it matter, if she had no way of ever going back? And where the hell was this thing taking her?

She killed her waking time by talking to the cobweb. It wasn't much of a conversationalist, but it learned to count eventually, and it could mimic anything she said. She named everything she could see out loud, which included body parts and stars and... that was it. She named the thing, officially, Cobweb.

And then, after countless sleeps, she finally woke to a horizon.

It was blue. The wrong blue. A gas giant orbiting a red sun. Clouds swirled and spun in lava lamp dances from pole to pole, turquoise and robin's egg and white. She watched it quietly, for hours, before naming it.

"Planet," she said.

"Planet," said Cobweb.

"Sorry I'm not more creative."

"Sorry I'm not more creative." She accepted its apology.

And just as a small, red-orange sphere rose over Planet's endless storms, she fell asleep again.

Dusty sand supported her when she woke, holding her hands and feet, arms and legs, neck and face against gravity. It felt strange to feel her weight again, and stranger to feel her face, nose and mouth buried in sand that didn't irritate her eyes or threaten to fill her lungs. Cobweb had set her face-down on this moon. How could it know she wasn't accustomed to slithering or rolling? It seemed to have simply dropped her in the position from which she was least likely to fall.

Inside the cobweb, she felt no difference between this atmosphere and empty space, and had no way of knowing if the air had oxygen, if it was cold, or what the wind felt like. She couldn't even taste the sand in her mouth. But at least it looked different.

She lay there for a moment, weakened by long-term weightlessness but also elated to be touching ground. Any ground. She couldn't feel the planet directly with her skin, but the cobweb was thin and she could feel the texture of the sand if she rubbed it between her fingers, the bumps of pebbles prodding her flesh.

When she did decide to stand, she realized she was far too weak. Everything had atrophied. And she was thin – emaciated, on the edge of starving. But not hungry. Cobweb made every molecule she needed, and nothing more.

"Come on, help me out. You brought us through Galaxy knows how much space but you can't help me stand up?"

"Come on, help me out..." Mindless repetition. She sighed.

The landscape reminded her of Mars. The odds were against this atmosphere being breathable by humans, but she had no way of knowing. She was in a space suit still — just a very thin, weirdly intelligent space suit that liked to kidnap exopaleontologists and happened to be equipped for interstellar travel.

Interstellar travel. The phrase echoed in her mind as her eyes followed the brownish-red horizon, the double-shadows of the rocks and dunes, and the blue giant in the sky whose reflected light made weak, blue double shadows. She was truly in another solar system.

Everyone... Julian, Linda, her crew, her parents... all gone with time. Julian's sobbing last words to her echoed across the plain. They were probably the last human words she would ever hear.

"Why did you bring me here?" she asked.

"Why did you bring me here?" Cobweb answered.

"Six days have passed," Cobweb told her the moment the red sun fell below the horizon. It was the first day it had told her on its own.

Valley smiled. It felt weird. She hadn't used her smile muscles in... how long?

The days were less objective than on Earth — she was on a moon, so there was the orbit of the moon around the blue gas giant she'd named Planet, and then there was the orbit of both bodies around the red sun. So some nights the gas giant was in the sky, and some nights it wasn't. And then there were eclipses, which were basically nights. All that considered, this moon's rotation felt like maybe half a day to Valley, and its orbit around Planet seemed only slightly longer. But she had no frame of reference except her own compromised biology.

"How many days since you kidnapped me?"

It echoed her, dumbly. She kept walking. It had learned how to support her weight and assist her movements, but nothing close to a concept as abstract as 'kidnap'. She didn't even know to explain 'take' without someone else from which to take something.

The sky was growing dark, but she wasn't tired and even if there was danger, there was no shelter. It really did remind her of Mars. A dead world. If Cobweb had creators, there was no evidence of them here.

She tripped over something, and fell hard into sand and rocks. "Dammit! Ow. You can protect me from the freezing vacuum of space but not from a stupid rock? Thanks a lot. Jerk."

It repeated everything back to her, including her childish outrage. She fumed silently while she picked herself up.

The rock she'd tripped over could just barely be made out in the light of the crescent blue giant.

Its edge was too straight. She dusted it off. Its right angles were worn smooth by wind, but it had definitely been rectangular once. Made of red sandstone.

There were more of them on either side of it and underneath. Identical.

She'd tripped over a wall.

Oh, hell. It thinks I'm an archaeologist. You and every cab driver and half my cousins.

"I'm a *paleontologist*, Cobweb. Exo-paleon-tologist."

And yet, looking over that worn right angle in the soft blue light, the magnitude of the discovery made her heart race. There could be fossils yet to be found.

Morning light revealed the outline of a buried city. She'd seen places like this as an undergrad, on the way to Mesozoic field sites in New Mexico. Unexcavated ruins, almost indistinguishable from the surrounding stone and sand until you start to see a pattern that nature doesn't make. Just take out all the sagebrush, and turn the sky a dusty orange, drop a blue gas giant in the sky and —

Holy shit, what is that? Something moved in the ruins and it wasn't masonry. A... blob... four or five times her size, lurched toward her.

It was wrapped in the same diaphanous material she was, grayish and shining gold where the sun hit it.

The blob had its own cobweb.

How long had it been here? How was it still alive? Where was it from? Was it dangerous? Was it intelligent?

It was shapeless, amorphous, moved like a galloping amoeba. It slowed as it came close, then stopped about four body lengths away from her. Was it afraid?

She waved. For a second she had a mental image of the naked couple on the Voyager plate and laughed — nervous, too loud — startling herself. The blob twitched.

It was flickering vivid purple patterns across its skin, under its cobweb.

"Blue," said Cobweb.

She shook her head. "Purple."

She looked down at her own body. Cobweb had perfectly matched the shade, on the outside. She was a vivid purple from head to toe.

She wanted to try something. "Red," she said. Her exterior turned red.

The blob lost its color. No red.

"Blue." She turned the precise color of the only blue around — the gas giant they orbited. The blob changed a dull purple.

Maybe it can only do purple, she thought. *Maybe most of its light perception is in the ultraviolet range, and I can't even see ninety percent of what it's showing me.*

She tried something else. "One." Cobweb drew one line, a photographic replica in purple of the ones she'd drawn in the sand, across her chest. "Two. Three. Four." Cobweb kept up, adding lines as she counted.

The blob matched her at four lines. Then showed her five. "Five!" she said, and Cobweb matched it. The blob showed a sixth. "Six!" Cobweb translated. Blob went to seven.

Excitedly, she said, "Planet!" Cobweb displayed a vivid, photographic rendition of what she'd seen in space as they approached this world. A screengrab from the moment she named it. She couldn't see it all, but suddenly her hands were covered with stars, her legs and belly were the blue of the gas giant, and rising behind it, across her chest, was the unmistakable red-brown surface of the moon that all four of them now shared — human, blob, and the cobwebs covering each. *Where's your 'Sorry I'm not more creative,' now?*

Blob displayed a similar image, but in shades of purple, and from a different angle of approach.

She clapped her hands with delight. In response, Blob protruded two pseudopods and tapped their ends together.

I've made friends with an alien!

They walked the ruins together, stopping to dig at interesting spots. The city had been huge, and they spent days exploring. Valley wondered at first if Blob was from this planet, maybe some more habitable region, and if Blob's people had created the cobwebs — assuming the cobwebs had creators at all. But the way Blob poked and prodded at the stones the same way she did, curiously searching these ruins as if this place were just as strange to them as it was to Valley, convinced her they were in the same boat she was. Alone and far from home, wondering why they were here.

Another intelligence with its own cobweb in the mix gave Cobweb the chance to learn more abstract concepts, like "us," "here," and "there." Blob expressed themselves in flashing purple patterns and bulbous protrusions, no sound. She wasn't sure if they had eyes, but they seemed to see in every direction at once.

"Having someone else here," she rambled, knowing nothing would translate but needing to talk, "someone I can look at, walk side by side with — probably ride, but that seems rude — and talk to, sort of, it's incredible. It's the best. It's like a new best friend on the first day of kindergarten. And..." she said the next line over Cobweb's mindless repetition, "It's so fucking lonely, too." The words were lost in Cobweb's echoes. When they finally repeated back, she cringed.

When it had just been her, she could forget.

Now, Blob reminded her of everyone else she'd ever walked with. Everyone who was gone. She found herself telling Blob about thunderstorms and coffee and the *Prince of Cats*, and even though Cobweb couldn't translate basically any of it and had no idea what the *Prince of Cats* or even Earth was, Valley would trail off mid-sentence, choking on a name whose face she was already forgetting.

"My chatter must sound like birdsong to you," she said to Blob.

"Birdsong?" Cobweb asked.

Blob flashed inscrutable purple patterns.

Maybe they were rambling, too.

Thinking of Cobweb's calibration sequence, Valley realized she and Blob had a lot in common. Considering the vast range of strengths of different frequencies — what if Blob's bioluminescence had blinded her? What if her voice had deafened them? What if she'd towered over them and accidentally stepped on them, or vice versa? Shit, had she stepped on anyone already? What other beings were out there? How many worlds with ruins? What other languages did the cobwebs know?

Blob and Valley operated at comparable time scales — although sometimes Blob made lightning quick pattern changes, like flipping through the pages of a book.

She imagined Blob giving up in those ruins where she'd found them. Wandering for months — years — being kept alive by their cobweb. How long had they been there, staring at the ruined walls? If she hadn't found Blob, Valley could see herself sitting down one day and letting the sand bury her. Was that what Blob had been doing when she found them?

Day twenty-one (so Cobweb announced at sunrise) arrived with a question. Cobweb might finally be ready to answer it. "How long has this been here?" she asked, then had to spend the morning teaching Cobweb "wall" and "city" and exponents.

The short answer, which took four hours to get to, was that Cobweb didn't know.

"Come on, you work at a molecular level, you create oxygen and amino acids on the fly! You're telling me you can't do some simple radiometric dating?"

And as Cobweb repeated back every part it was confused about, which was all of it, she realized she would need to find something organic, or some material that had crystallized the same time the city was constructed. Glass might work. Masonry would only give the date the rocks were formed, and sandstone masonry would only give the date of the rock its sand was made of... and as she recited the fundamentals of her profession to herself, she had flashbacks to freshman geoscience... and for some reason that TA, Miranda, the one she'd had a crush on... and then she started to cry again.

Fuck this planet.

She yelled the thought as loud as she could, and kicked the sand.

Blob came up to her, protruded a lump near their base, and kicked the sand with it.

Valley was startled to hear her own laughter.

Excavating became their life. They conversed in purple shapes and sand drawings, while digging and digging and digging. Valley dug with her hands, Cobweb reinforcing them into trowels, and Blob moved vast amounts of sand with a shovel-shaped pseudopod. Valley drew when they got tired. She taught Blob and Cobweb the alphabet, the positions of the stars she remembered from her own sky, silly symbols like hearts and smiley faces. She tried to teach Cobweb the different emotions, but it only seemed to understand them as chemical signals, which, when she thought about it, they were.

While Blob could replicate her sand drawings with perfect purple accuracy, Valley had no way of reproducing Blob's flashing patterns. She would have to name the patterns she noticed, tell Cobweb the name, and have Cobweb display it back to Blob. But she never noticed the same thing twice. Maybe the meaningful parts were outside her visible spectrum, faster than she could observe, or maybe her brain just wasn't built to recognize them. They would have to create a shared language in the media they had in common. Maybe their cobwebs could do the rest, eventually.

Cobweb now understood, at least sometimes, the difference between a statement and a question. That meant she could ask it things, and she discovered it was able to answer in pictures, displayed just in front of her eyes, in a kind of cave-painting-and-photograph head-up display. "Where is Blob?" returned a photographic rendition of Blob next to a rock or wherever they happened to be at that moment.

She drew her ship. The *Prince of Cats*. She made it as detailed as possible. Blob watched intently in their eyeless, faceless way, and displayed a perfect rendition of her drawing back to her, as creases and ridges in dust, sprawled life-size across their skin. She wondered if they even understood it as symbolic, or if they thought she was just playing in the dirt.

She looked intently at her masterpiece, and said, "*Prince of Cats.*"

"*Prince of Cats*," Cobweb agreed.

"Picture. Use picture." It obliged by showing her a perfect photograph of what she had just drawn, the same as Blob had done.

"Show me things like this that you and I have seen together." It displayed a series of rocks, patterns in the sand, features on hillsides. She kept shaking her head. Finally it showed a comet — a KBO? — that vaguely resembled the outline. Maybe it was going back in time.

There it was! "Yes! The *Prince of Cats!* Yes!" It held the image. She felt her eyes make tears at the sight of it, and she felt Cobweb absorb them before they could fall. The *Prince of Cats* was beautiful. It had been her home for two years. She'd done the most important work of her career inside that tin can.

Her throat knotted. The *Prince of Cats* was long gone. Its crew were dust.

Had they made it home? Had Istry finished his book? Had Omar ever asked Reed out? Had Julian ever forgiven himself for forgetting her tether? And Linda — that psycho. Had her investors been happy when the *Prince of Cats* returned down a crew member but up an observation? Had they ever figured out what the cobwebs were?

And her mom and dad. Had they coped...? *Oooh, Mom. I'm so sorry. Daddy...*

She stared into the sand. Were there more grains or regrets?

"How long has it been?" she asked, her voice choking up with chemical signals that only she knew were emotions.

"One thousand and twelve days," it answered.

How... Wait what?

She tried to guess how many Earth days that was. Maybe two years? How could that be possible? The *Prince of Cats* would barely be back near Saturn Station.

She needed to share this with Blob.

"Show the *Prince of Cats* to Blob," she told it. Blob displayed it back to her instantaneously, then surprised her by overlaying her sand drawing on top of it. It was all in shades of violet. She nodded and smiled. Blob protruded a bulbous appendage that nodded back at her.

"Tell Blob it's been one thousand and twelve days since we saw the *Prince of Cats*."

Blob flashed violet patterns. They seemed contemplative.

"Cobweb, do you think Blob's species hugs?"

This of course was too abstract, even if Cobweb had any way of knowing what a hug was. Anyway, she didn't want to make Blob uncomfortable. So she drew a heart in the sand.

There must be something they were meant to find here, on this planet, some reason their cobwebs had brought them here.

The scientist in her kept digging, counting, drawing symbols in the sand.

One evening, when the blue giant had eclipsed its sun and the sky was filled with bright strange stars, Blob showed her their own ship. A purple cylinder floating in a purple star field appeared across their skin. The image panned around the ship, and then zoomed in on a star behind it. They'd composed a whole video.

"Is that your sun?" Their cobwebs translated what they could of the question from her sound into Blob's violet patterns, and Blob nodded a protrusion. She wasn't convinced they'd understood her question, though. Cobweb was still finding possessives a challenge.

"You're homesick." There was no translation. She tried something else. *"Prince of Cats."* Cobweb displayed her ship. Blob nodded.

Valley fell asleep staring up at the endless stars, filled with hopeless frustration she didn't know how to express.

It was a bright day. The sky was less dusty than usual and Planet was so crisp on the horizon she could see its clouds.

A good day for an abstract concept.

"Show Blob over by that wall," she said. Cobweb knew which wall she meant because she was looking at it; she didn't even need to gesture. Although to

Cobweb, she supposed, a glance was just a gesture with a small wet body part.

It displayed an image of Blob near the wall. She got excited. Blob was not currently near the wall. They were right there in front of her.

Blob seemed excited too. They flashed purple, then, to her surprise and delight, lurched their way toward the wall, and stopped right where the image had shown them. She clapped her hands and nodded.

Blob nodded in response and clapped protrusions, then lurched back toward her.

An idea came to her as they approached, one of those ideas so obvious in retrospect you can't help but laugh to yourself out loud, and Valley did.

Cobweb had brought her here to meet Blob, not find the ruins. There was nothing in the ruins.

It had landed her near Blob and subtly directed her to Blob's location because their communication systems were so compatible. Or perhaps Blob was just the closest sentient lifeform of any kind. Either way — the goal of the cobwebs was to make introductions. That had to be it.

Perhaps Cobweb had not, after all, mistaken her for an exoarchaeologist. Of course they'd found nothing in the ruins. The ruins were incidental. They were meant to find each other.

Back at her side, Blob displayed an image of Valley standing by a large rock, about thirty feet away.

It was the first time she'd seen herself since she was on board the *Prince of Cats*. She was thrilled to see a human form, though it was purple, covered in the skintight cobweb, hairless and emaciated and effectively nude. She wondered briefly what non-living accessories Blob had started out with. She didn't know how to ask. Fur? Scales? A carapace? Clothes? Integument came in so many forms.

She stood up and walked over to the rock, just where Blob had shown her. Blob flashed purple, nodded and clapped. Valley did the same, except the purple part, and ran back over to Blob.

She grabbed a rock. "Take this over to the wall," she said. Cobweb didn't know what to make of "take this", but showed her the rock at the wall. "Show Blob and the rock at the wall." It obliged.

Blob protruded a limb toward her. She held out the rock in her hand. "Take," she said, as Blob picked up the rock from the palm of her hand.

"Take," Cobweb repeated.

Blob lurched back to the wall, and gently set the rock down at its base, where Cobweb had shown it.

She clapped and nodded.

Now for the real test. Cobweb had taken her light years against her will. Could it take her twenty feet on command? "Cobweb. Take Valley to the wall."

She felt her arms and legs move without her control. It was more terrifying than she thought it would be, but she tried to relax and let Cobweb move her. It was not unlike the way it assisted her movements normally, but totally giving up control was disconcerting and she kept tensing up involuntarily.

The movements were slow and jerky. Halfway there she felt a muscle cramp up, and her leg stiffened. Cobweb stopped its motions and she fell over. Blob rushed to her side. They couldn't possibly understand that she was in pain, but they surely recognized motions that were unusual for her. Did they guess what she was trying to do?

Blob helped her up. She wondered again if their species hugged.

"How could I leave you alone here? We still have so much to learn about each other."

The next morning, when she was fully awake and sitting up in the sand, trying to remember what coffee tasted like, Blob approached her. They displayed their purple cylinder ship in its purple sky, extended a protrusion, and gently touched her arm. On the protrusion was an image of a heart, drawn in lavender sand.

Then Blob collapsed into a crumpled piece of laundry.

Their cobweb was empty.

"Blob?"

It ruffled slightly in the wind.

"No, no, no... Blob?? *Blob?!*" She crouched and reached toward the cobweb, then stopped short of grabbing it. It looked so fragile.

In the right environment, the empty, crumpled cobweb might, over time, be preserved between layers of sediment, and flattened into a fossil like the one she and Julian had found on that meteorite on Titan. The one she'd written her thesis on. The one that had started all this bullshit.

The one that, eventually, had led her here, to Blob.

"Cobweb. Where is Blob?" She could hear the panic in her voice. Old terror crept back into her stomach, that fear of being eaten alive, the memory of the certainty of death when her helmet first caved in under the thousand microscopic mouths of a grey-gold film in space.

Cobweb displayed an arrow drawn in sand, a photographic replica of one she'd drawn when teaching it directions. It pointed up and to the left. Her eyes followed it until it hovered over a nondescript spot in the bright, dust-filled sky.

She remembered Blob's last message. The image of their ship.

"Cobweb, what happened to Blob?"

"Blob is not here."

"Damn it, Cobweb, I need a better answer! Is Blob hurt?"

"Blob is not hurt."

"Can I see Blob?"

"Can I see?" Cobweb didn't understand.

"Show me Blob." Cobweb showed Blob as they'd looked right in front of her the moment before they disappeared.

She sat in the sand and dropped her face into her hands.

Blob had left her alone, with only Cobweb and the silent ghosts of this nameless, galaxy-forsaken moon.

She woke in a dust storm. Cobweb protected her skin and eyes, but she couldn't see anything and didn't feel like doing anything even if she could have. She lay in the sand and let the dust cover her.

How many sentient beings were buried in cobwebs on ruined worlds?

She thought of the first time she'd met Blob, the way they moved toward her — excitedly, she now realized — across those ruins. The first time Blob touched two pseudopods together after she clapped her hands. She thought of Blob's excited purple flashing, and their shared moment of discovery when they taught their cobwebs 'take'.

Had Blob told their cobweb to take them away? To take them home? Could it be that simple? But how had they travelled? It had seemed instantaneous, and Blob had left their cobweb behind.

Maybe Blob's species had some trick? Maybe they'd been rescued somehow?

Then another thought occurred to her. "Cobweb," she whispered, "take me to Blob's cobweb."

She blacked out.

When she woke, the dust storm still raged but the sand under her had shifted. She felt around. It wasn't anywhere in front of her.

She sat up. A crumpled, empty cobweb was just behind her, laying in the center of a human-shaped depression in the sand.

"Incredible," she whispered. That wasn't Blob's cobweb. It was hers. She was *in* Blob's cobweb now. It felt identical.

"How many cobwebs have I had?"

"Three thousand nine hundred and twenty nine."

It was her own voice, just like her cobweb had used. She'd realized the cobwebs must share information from the way they facilitated her and Blob's communication, but now it was obvious they were more intricately networked. They didn't just transmit information.

They transmitted matter. That was why they didn't need propulsion. That was how they kept her and Blob alive on a planet that had only rocks and air.

There could be trillions of them. They could be in every solar system in the galaxy, undetected by civilizations like her own until adventurers like Julian and Linda and herself — and Blob — journeyed to their comet belts, where the cobwebs grazed and left trace fossils between accretion layers.

Blob had figured it all out, but hadn't known how to tell her. They could only show her by example.

And Cobweb. All the cobwebs. They couldn't just plant her on some inhabited world and expect the natives to treat her with respect — no, they had done this many times and knew how fucked up social species could be. They had to make introductions on worlds where two beings would be forced to become friends.

It had worked.

She thought of her ship mates. Linda's constant string of profanity, which had apparently rubbed off on Valley more than she'd realized, and the rest of the crew — Istry with his dark sexy shoulders and quiet hours writing. Omar and Reed's constant flirtation in the engine room. And Julian. Stupid, space-mad Julian who'd gotten her into this mess in the first place with a forgotten tether.

I am gonna kick your ass for this, Julian. ...After hugging you really, really hard.

Valley closed her eyes. It seemed like a good time for a deep breath, but she hadn't breathed in months, so she shrugged instead. *No way is this going to work.*

"Cobweb. Take me to the *Prince of Cats*."

And the red world faded, and she fell asleep.

No spacesuit was needed. She floated outside the hull of the *Prince of Cats*, a layer thin as breath between her skin and the void. She was Valley, and she was Cobweb, and she was something else.

She'd come out here, to the Kuiper Belt, to find a fossil. Now she had a universe to share. A species of Blobs to introduce them to. A story that actually involved space archaeology, for all those distant relatives who only half-remembered her profession.

Someone noticed her through the window of the starboard cupola. Linda. A coffee mug fell from her hand, brown liquid splashed against the pane. Her mouth formed the shape of a four letter word. She turned and shouted to someone out of view.

"Cobweb, are you picking up any radio signals?"

"Radio signals?"

Oh, there was still so much to teach this thing.

Someone else appeared in the window, next to Linda. It was Julian. He held up a piece of paper, letters hastily scrawled.

VALLEY?!!

"Valley," said Cobweb.

She nodded. "Would you write something back to him for me, Cobweb?" She spelled it out, and the letters appeared across her torso, replicas of ones she'd drawn in sand.

I'M OK!

NEED HUGS THO.

She wondered, as the airlock door inched open, if there was any hot coffee left. And then a terrifying thought occurred to her. What if she couldn't taste it?

See Thea Boodhoo's story "A Layer Thin As Breath" online at Metaphorosis.
If you liked it, leave a comment. Authors love that!
Remember to subscribe to our e-mail updates so you'll know when new stories are posted.

About the story

About seven years ago, I decided it was time to read Asimov. Somewhere deep into the *Foundation* series, I felt inspired to create a short story in his style, which seemed to rely on all the action happening in meetings where people sitting around conference tables had heated conversations about what other people were doing in space. That story turned into the better part of a novel, and that novel sat around in a drawer for a few years while I focused on non-fictional science communication. When I finally had the courage to start writing science fiction again, I took my favorite part of the novel, which wasn't Asimovian at all, and turned it into a short story.

"A Layer Thin As Breath" is heavily informed by my interest in different intelligences and what it might take to communicate with them. I gave a talk, and later wrote an essay, on this topic called "UX for Aliens", which you can still read on my website, theaboodhoo.com. I largely blame Irene Pepperberg for this interest, whose work with parrots I read about at the impressionable age of 15, as well as a woman I once knew who claimed to have known a space alien rather well, and my dad, whose college girlfriend was a dolphin.

A question for the author

Q: Have you ever consciously written a 'message' story? Was it easier or harder than usual?

A: The most popular thing I've written to date is called "Open letter to the tech bro who spat at me, from that pigeon eating a noodle on Market Street." I wrote it after seeing a man spit at a pigeon. It took me forty-five minutes and was fueled by pure rage. I don't know if I'll ever be able to write something like that again. The message was: don't be a dick to pigeons.

About the author

Thea Boodhoo grew up in the western United States as the only child of bohemian intellectuals. The only hobbies she could afford were free ones, so she became a writer and explorer. The redwood forest and the high desert were her best friends — and maybe they still are. She lives in San Francisco with an old shaggy rabbit, a looming jungle of houseplants, and thirty reference books on indigenous foods for her in-progress science fiction novel.

theaboodhoo.com, @tharkibo

Communication Breakdown

Andrew Knighton

"No." I pushed my chair back from the conference table. I could see myself in the window opposite, Herrje's deep night sky turning the glass wall into a giant mirror. Beyond that window was one of the most amazing cities in the universe, a melting pot in which dozens of races and cultures mixed, their mingled architectural styles creating a cityscape like no other. But all I could see was myself, looking angry and in need of a shave. "No sodding way."

Thea Canning peered at me across her glasses. The British ambassador in Herrje was used to arguing with alien species, not her own staff. She nearly managed to hide her surprise behind her inexpressive face and sharply tailored suit.

"This is going to happen, Julian." She was still using my first name. I wasn't in trouble yet. "Britain needs this peace. Earth needs this peace."

"Earth doesn't need me for it." I stared at the jar on the table, which everyone else seemed so blasé about. An inch-long black parasite writhed inside it like an excitable slug. The sight was stomach-churning. "Let someone else play host to the Veng."

It was easy for me to say that. I hadn't lost anyone I cared about in the war, because there were so few people I even halfway liked. But Canning had lost a brother fighting for the outer colonies; Warren, our security officer, had been a marine in the lunar landings; even Hannah, my placid assistant, got nervous when messages came in from her sister in the RAF. As the three of them stared at me, I could feel the pressure of their collective need.

Of everyone in this room, I was the one with least at stake, and I was the one being asked to pay the price.

"You are our communications officer," Canning said.

"That means I do public relations, not body swaps."

"Mister Atticus, you speak thirteen languages and have spent time with a score of different races. You are the ideal choice for this task."

"But this task is a terrible choice for me." I pressed a hand against my chest. "I love my body. I don't want to have it violated by that thing."

"Don't try that "my body is a temple" nonsense with me." Canning tapped a finger against the table. "You eat like a horse and you haven't been to the gym in months."

"I have a job to do, briefings to deliver, press releases to write."

"You work for me, and as of right now this is part of your job. Given the PR blackout around the negotiations, there's nothing on your plate that Hannah can't handle. Isn't that right, Hannah?"

"I'd be honoured to do it," Hannah said brightly.

I glared at her. "Kiss arse."

Her face fell.

"I'm only trying to help," she said, staring at her hands.

Of course she was. Hannah was far too sweet to be stuck as my emotional punchbag, but PR was too harsh a world to start pulling my blows.

I looked at the jar again. On the inside of my contact lenses, a readout provided facts about Veng biology, such as how they laid their eggs and how much mucus they secreted in a week. The thought of swallowing all that slime and tentacles made me shudder.

"This must be a violation of my human rights," I said.

Canning sighed. "Are you really going to try that one on?"

"No." I slumped in my seat.

"Good. Now open wide and swallow the Veng emissary."

"This isn't fair!" Even I was embarrassed by my petulance.

"Life is not fair, Mister Atticus. We make of it what we can."

She took the lid off the jar and pushed it towards me. The Veng representative raised the part of itself that came closest to a head – a cluster of tiny, writhing limbs. It wasn't even a conscious being in its own right, just an appendage of a portion of a vast collective intelligence, one of many that shared Veng space. I reached in and picked it up, my skin crawling as it pulsed beneath my fingertips.

I gave Canning one last pleading look, then tipped my head back and dropped the Veng into my mouth. It squirmed for a moment and then writhed at alarming speed back along my tongue. I gagged, then choked, then almost vomited as it wriggled down my throat and into my belly.

I couldn't feel it anchoring itself within me, or the tendrils that reached out to tap into my nervous system. What I felt was a coldness spreading through my guts, and tangled, nonsensical thoughts spilling across my brain, images that were not my own. Far away creatures and places that made me sigh wistfully even though I had never been there. I slumped in my seat as a sudden lethargy overtook me.

"Good man," Canning said. "And remember, caffeine disrupts the mental bond, so no coffee until this is done."

I was still half present for the initial negotiations the next day, listening numbly as the Veng consciousness used the parasite to control my body, my mouth conveying its message, my eyes and ears taking in the response. There was talk of reparations, border demarcations, and future trade relations, setting out the crude picture which the next few days would refine.

I had hundreds of questions about what was happening to me and no chance to ask any of them. Instead, I sat like a passenger in my own body, brooding on how I could avoid having to do this again – a career change, a better assistant, perhaps some sort of drug problem that would make my body unusable. It wasn't exactly productive, but what else was I going to do?

I watched events around me as if they were happening on a distant screen. The longer the talks went on, the further I drifted, greyness descending like the gentle touch of sleep. I was aware of Hannah giving my shoulder a reassuring squeeze and of Canning's look of approval. After that, it was someone else's life.

I had known in advance that there were going to be blackouts. You don't play host to another consciousness and always get to be yourself.

What I didn't expect was to be left hungover.

The first time was fine. I lost two days, then found myself sitting back in the conference room, mouth dry and head fuzzy, Canning giving me an uncertain look.

"That is you, isn't it, Julian?" she said.

I nodded, blinked, and looked around, assessing my environment as I pulled my consciousness back together.

"I thought so. There's a different look to those eyes when they belong to the Veng."

"Belong," I said with a frown. "Huh."

I didn't like the idea of belonging to anyone. Even my loyalty is my own, not the property of His Majesty's Government.

"The talks seem to be going well," Canning said. "How does it look from the other side?"

"No idea." My thoughts came slowly, as if I had had just one too many drinks the previous night. It seemed that downing a Veng was not so different from downing tequila shots – there was the same memory loss and the same aftermath of distant and unaccountable sadness, but with less of a headache.

I reached for the coffee pot in the middle of the table, then remembered the sacrifices I was making and slammed the pot back down.

"As I said when you first fielded this plan, the talk of "shared consciousness" is a mistranslation," I said. "That idiot Hemming can barely get French right, never mind Veng. This isn't a team-up. The brain slug replaces me."

"That's a shame," Canning said, her brow crumpling. "I had hoped to gain some insider insight, but at least you get to feel vindicated."

"What a huge comfort."

"It's better than nothing." She smiled slightly. "Alright, you go rest. And you might want to check in with Hannah – she's been worried about you."

"All the more reason not to see her." I didn't want to encourage my assistant's personal interest in me. In less senior company I would have said as much, and not politely. But Canning, as well as my boss, was a smart lady who could read between the lines.

"Go," she said. "Sleep."

I went back to my room, had a shower and a meal – carefully avoiding any trace of caffeine – and waited for the thing to take over again. Normally when I was that tense I would have put on a porn movie and given myself some biological relaxation, but the thought of someone else turning up in my body mid-wank was just too embarrassing.

The second time around was different. I woke up in my usual slacks and black shirt, but this time I was in bed. The damned slug hadn't bothered getting undressed.

"What is this bullshit?" I shouted, leaping to my feet. The room spun around me and I collapsed back in a heap.

I smelt like a nightclub toilet, all stale booze, week-old sweat and dead cigarettes. My head was pounding – part pain, part the sound of knocking on my door. According to the digits on the inside of my contact lens, a week had passed.

Strangely, I didn't feel like I'd had a lot of fun. The Veng was somewhere in the back of my brain, looking out through my eyes, but there was no joy in it, just a sense of distance, even disappointment, as if it had turned up to a much-anticipated party and found that it didn't like the rest of the guests. And for some reason, my arm was aching.

I crawled out of bed, moving more carefully this time, and pulled myself upright using the bookcase in the corner of the room. Someone had emptied all the bottles from the top shelf, leaving only the dregs of something sickly in the bottom of the cocktail shaker. I staggered to the door and swung it open.

Hannah looked up at me with big, concerned eyes. I sighed. I did not want to be doing this.

"Are you alright, Mister Atticus?" She gestured towards a stain on the carpet. "Warren said you were bleeding when you came in."

I rolled up the sleeve of my aching arm and looked down at a thick, ugly scab.

"What the…?"

My pulse quickened as I stared at the wound. That bastard Veng had done this, and not even bothered to get it treated.

"The ambassador wants to see you," Hannah said.

"The ambassador can sod off," I snapped.

Hannah took a step back, lip trembling, and some of my fury turned inward. This wasn't her fault, it was the Veng's.

"Can I shower first?" I asked.

"The ambassador called you Mister Atticus."

"You call me Mister Atticus."

"But I think it's a nice name."

I sighed and followed Hannah out of the room. The door closed behind me, its click like a dagger in my skull. In the back of my mind, the Veng was feeling sorry for itself, but I didn't think that was about how it had messed with me. The bastard was in a sulk and I was on the receiving end.

When I got to Canning's office, with its empty desk and plain walls, the ambassador was stood by the window, looking out across the skyline of Herrje. It was a spectacularly eclectic sight, human skyscrapers standing amidst the vaulted arches of the shoji sector, low groundling domes running up against the battered blocks of the k'kiri markets. I might get frustrated at this place, angry even, but I never got bored.

"Close the door," Canning said.

I turned to obey. Warren, the head of security, was there ahead of me. Gone was his usual affectation of a twentieth century tie. At least he still wore the smugness he showed whenever I was in trouble.

I sank into a chair. My stomach sank with me.

"Where have you been?" Canning turned to face me. She held a cup of coffee, the most delicious thing I had ever smelled. Between the hangover and a fortnight without caffeine, I would have killed for a cup, but just thinking that set the Veng writhing angrily inside me.

"Where have you been?" she repeated as I stared slack-jawed at her cup.

"I don't know," I said, snapping back to reality. "Isn't it Warren's job to keep track of me and my passenger?"

"You lost him three days ago," she said. "After a particularly fruitless day of negotiations. It's almost as if the Veng don't want peace."

It was a chilling thought. The war hadn't been lost, but there was no doubting that we had suffered the most. If the Veng decided to push on, thousands more soldiers would be joining Canning's brother in floating mausoleums far from home.

She sipped at the coffee and narrowed her gaze as she watched my reaction. Was she still hoping that I would remember something the alien had thought?

"Maybe they don't want peace." It was a dark idea, but I was in a dark place, full of the hollowness that follows an epic night out. I'd put my body through some hellish hangovers, but none that left me as despondent as I felt now, with the tendrils of Veng thought trailing through my brain.

"They put too much effort into making this happen," Canning said. "Even choosing a fragment of a Veng consciousness to send took weeks. Something else is going on."

"I pity the poor Veng that got stuck with this job," I said. "When you're used to sharing in a collective consciousness, it's got to be lonely only having a single human's thoughts for company."

"Especially when that human's you," Warren said.

I ignored the taunt, closed my eyes, and tried to feel the Veng's presence in my mind. It did seem a little sad, though that could just have been home sickness or a hangover. I wondered what was getting to it and whether there was anything I could do to help. With a little effort, maybe I could bridge the gap between us and be a better host.

"Shit!" I jumped as Warren stuck a needle in my arm, pulled it out and read the syringe's electronic display.

"How sexually active are you, Atticus?" He looked up from the readout with a grin.

"Far less than I'd like." I stared despondently at the syringe. Was my parasite getting lucky behind my back? "Tell me the worst."

"K'kiri vein crabs." Warren passed the syringe to Canning. "A couple of psychotropic drugs too. Your body's been living the high life."

"I didn't think you could catch vein crabs off humans." The ambassador put down her coffee and examined the syringe.

"You can't," I said, frozen in my seat. Now I was glad for the mercy of full blackout. Inter-alien fun-times might be a turn-on for some people, but I was a one species man. I felt violated in the worst possible way.

"Increase the guards," Canning said to Warren. "We need to get these negotiations on track."

"Whoah whoah whoah!" I staggered red-faced to my feet. "I've been turned into a pervert by the damn Veng brain slug. You're getting it out of me, right?"

"Once we're done."

"Screw that." I had to do something to avoid another takeover. Still befuddled, I snatched the coffee cup and downed its lukewarm contents.

The scab on my arm cracked, blood dripping on the carpet. Canning looked at me with cold, dead eyes.

"Pray that does not cause a problem, Mister Atticus," she said. "Warren, lock down the east wing apartments. He won't be going out."

I woke to the strangest sensation. I'd been dreaming about having sex with Hannah, her pasty little body wobbling around beneath me. As consciousness took hold, I could feel myself moving on her still, and then I realised that my eyes were open.

Oh sweet horror, it was real.

I tried to jerk away but my body wouldn't respond. I could feel someone else in there with me, grinding away in a desperate hunt for a pleasure it barely felt. A half-empty bottle of whiskey lay beside the bed and the room smelled of pot. Someone was having a wild time, and they were using my body to do it.

"Oh, yes," Hannah gasped. "Oh Julian, you don't know how long I've wanted this."

This was bad. This was very, very bad.

Not the sex itself. What I felt through the dreamlike haze was surprisingly good.

Not the weed and the booze either, though I wished I'd been around to enjoy the high.

No, doing this with Hannah was bad. The admin pool had bets on when I'd give in and hook up with her. Warren had sworn to break my legs if I broke her heart. I didn't want to be with my soppy, soft-hearted assistant, and yet some treacherous part of me was enjoying this.

Screw Canning's failed negotiations, this was my diplomatic hell.

I tried again to take control of my body, but the Veng sensed me now. It paused in its activities and I could feel its attention bearing down on me. Its thoughts whirled through the same space as my own. I struggled to make sense of the words and images, too wild and disjointed to have meaning for me, and I could sense a similar frustration on its part.

Frustration. I might not recognise its thoughts, but I recognised its feelings.

I probed deeper. There was loneliness, disappointment, a grey fog of loss all revolving around this time with me. The highs it had sought were nothing compared with the lows of being here. The poor bastard.

As I stared into the alien's feelings its gaze was drawn there too, sucking it deeper into its own depression. I let it ride that desolation, let it wallow, and took the moment to take control.

"Julian?" Hannah looked up at me uncertainly, raised a hand to stroke my face. "Julian, is something the matter?"

I got to my feet, stumbled naked and woozy towards the kitchen. The damn thing had been fighting deep sorrow, cut off from the rest of its hive mind just as I had been from my body. But how much whiskey had it drunk trying to cheer itself up?

Enough was enough. I needed this thing out.

I moved for the kettle, but there wasn't time. The Veng mind was stirring in me again, trying to take control. Tentacles of desperation battled with my own determination to be free.

"Julian?" Hannah rose. "Julian, what's the matter?"

No time. I yanked the fridge open, grabbed a bag of coffee beans and tipped them into my mouth. I chewed those acrid brown seeds like they were candy. They popped and crunched, and I swallowed the jagged, caffeinated shards. Chewed and swallowed, chewed and swallowed, the caffeine buzz breaking the Veng's hold.

In the last moment of connection, it seemed to be pleading with me, reaching out for something I didn't understand. Tears ran down my face and I sobbed at the terrible loneliness of it all.

My stomach lurched. I fell to my knees, vomiting up coffee grounds and the black, slug-like blob of the Veng.

Hannah crouched beside me, rubbing my back.

"It'll be OK," she murmured. "Whatever it is, it'll be OK."

I leaned in towards her, and it felt surprisingly good.

"That's it?" Canning asked.

I nodded and sipped at my tea.

"Separation from the hive took away all its pleasure," I said, peering at the slug-like blob in its jar on the desk. I felt sorry for it now, having felt what it did during those final shared moments in my room. But unlike the Veng, I was glad not to have anyone else in my thoughts. "Must be something to do with human bodies, or a lifetime of dousing myself with coffee. Once it realised, it spent the whole time seeking other thrills. Send it back. It'll be so relieved we'll have peace within days."

"Without a host, we can't talk with them." Canning frowned and tapped a finger on her desk.

"We don't need to," I said with confidence. "After that experience, they won't want anything we've got."

Canning turned toward Warren. For all his petty failings – and there were many of them – even I acknowledged that he knew security issues.

"Makes sense, given their other priorities," he growled, giving me the filthiest look I've ever received. "It's not like the talks were working."

"Very well." Canning turned from us back to her computer. "Thank you, gentlemen."

We rose to leave.

"I warned you, Atticus," Warren said as he followed to the door. "You hurt Hannah and now I'm going to break both your legs."

As we stepped out of the office, Hannah appeared and took my arm. Warren glared. I smiled and kissed the top of Hannah's head.

"We're off out for dinner," I said. "Don't wait up."

I didn't turn to see his expression, just enjoyed the feeling of having my thoughts to myself and of having Hannah beside me. Alone in my head, but not in the world.

See Andrew Knighton's story "Communication Breakdown" online at Metaphorosis.
If you liked it, leave a comment. Authors love that!
Remember to subscribe to our e-mail updates so you'll know when new stories are posted.

About the story

This story started with a character.

I created Julian Atticus years ago, for a short story called "Our Man in Herrje" that appeared in Jupiter SF. The story was about the difficulties of communicating with someone whose language and world view are completely alien to yours, specifically a species who hate lies. Working in PR, Atticus's propensity for lying got him into deep trouble with the aliens as he tried to disentangle a potential diplomatic disaster. It's a story I enjoyed writing, which made me fond of the character, and so I kept thinking about him.

Since then, I've returned to Julian Atticus several times. Bitter and jaded, he lets out a side of me that I usually conceal, and that can be incredibly cathartic. He's become my go-to guy for exploring the difficulties of communication, not just with aliens but with other humans and even with ourselves. Communication Breakdown was an attempt to present him with a whole new challenge - a species that needed a human host to communicate at all.

This story also digs into another theme that's close to my heart - loss of control. Working with others means letting go of control sometimes, but losing control of your own body is a terrifying thought. It's doubly so for someone as controlling and self-contained as Atticus. It was interesting to explore how he would react when his body stopped being his own. How would he cope with that change? Could he find a way to communicate with the alien within? And what might he learn from not being himself?

Communication is difficult. Miscommunication can be a great cause of conflict. Perhaps that's why, time after time, Julian Atticus keeps raising his voice to be heard - the other being sharing my body.

A question for the author

Q: Are you an outline or discovery writer?

A: I'm very much an outline writer. I like to think through where the story and the character are going before I get started. I might make changes along the way, but I find that structure is vital in freeing up my brain to focus on the words.

About the author

Andrew is a British ghostwriter, who pays his way by writing books and articles in other people's names. He lives in Yorkshire with his cat, his computer, and a huge pile of unread books. When he's not writing, he enjoys board games, bouldering, and trying to get through that pile of books.

andrewknighton.com, @gibbondemon

The Offshore

Josh Taylor

Jesper Torus had been standing on the same spot on the sidewalk for almost thirty minutes. The building in front of him was older but well-maintained, with marble latticework and gold-tipped iron railings on the terraces. He held up the letter with both hands. His fingers had left dark smudges, and dried sweat curled the corners. This was the right address. Women in makeup and clean-shaven men walked in and out, chatting energetically, striding with purpose. He drew in a breath and started toward the entrance.

No one stopped him in the lobby. He almost wished someone would, so everyone else would stop staring. In the elevator they held fingers under noses, in the hallway they dropped conversations and went to call security.

Glass-walled offices and landscape prints led up to a heavy wooden door. A tarnished bronze nameplate said 'Heggle Haulage.' Jesper pictured a torture dungeon on the other side. The door creaked open before he could knock, and closed behind him just as a guard emerged from the elevator.

Inside was a single enormous office. It wasn't well lit despite an encompassing grid of windows that arched into the ceiling, like in an old train station. More than a dozen leather couches formed several nooks for conversation. In the center stood a taxidermied elephant, ears outspread and trunk low, ready to charge.

"I'd invite you to sit, but then I'd have to buy a new couch."

Jesper mumbled, "Sorry," and began to shuffle towards the door.

"I didn't say to leave." An older man stepped out from behind a wooden desk. He had white hair and wore a purple linen shirt with gold cufflinks. Wrinkles webbed the skin around his eyes, evidently the result of a lifetime of gentle smiling. "I invited you here."

Jesper crinkled the letter in his hand.

"So you know who I am."

Jesper stared at the floor, unworthy, and mumbled, "Harg Heggle."

"That's right." Harg patted his desk. It was broad and solid, with clawed feet and carved ivy patterns curling down the legs. "You made this, you know."

At that, Jesper looked up. He squinted, looked away. The memories brought no pleasure.

"Sixty thousand, which was quite expensive at the time."

Jesper fumbled for another apology.

"I don't regret it, obviously." Harg ran his finger along the elephant's side as he approached. "Back then everyone had to have a Jesper Torus dinner table, or a Jesper Torus bedroom set, or Jesper Torus bunk beds for their kids and grandkids. Your prices were our favorite part. Now I prefer antiques, and you're of course out of business."

Jesper returned his gaze to the floor. He felt a pang of shame at the sight of his toe through his shoe.

Harg sat on the couch nearest Jesper and crossed his legs. "Homeless, by the stench."

Someone had to point it out to him at least once a day. "Why am I here?"

"A second chance."

Jesper flinched at the memory of his last second chance.

Harg continued, "Three years ago you used a shell corporation in the Cayman Islands to hide two million in a Swiss bank account. It was Jesla who helped you set it up, right? Or am I misremembering?"

Jesper nodded.

"Odd." There was an edge of impatience in Harg's voice. "I don't usually misremember."

Jesper coughed. He usually felt the need to cough before speaking. "It was Jesla."

Jesla Jimenez, metal mogul, had been so impressed with her new sapele entertainment unit that she'd opened up some rare bottle of scotch and given Jesper a free tutorial in shell corporations. It had all sounded so simple. Jesper had no competitors, not at his level of quality. Demand was soaring. Later that year he was going to open a third showroom and automate the factory's loading dock. "For people like us," Jesla had said, slightly drunk, squeezing his shoulder, "it just makes sense."

Jesper nodded again, coughed again. "Jimenez."

"Thought so," Harg chuckled. "That was exactly one month before the ratification of the International Open Banking Accord."

"I know I was wrong. Knew. So I don't get a second chance."

"They had to make an example of someone. Better you than Jesla, or me." Harg smiled. The corners of his eyes folded into grandfatherly wrinkles. "I'd say you were unlucky. And honest, I reckon, in spite of it all."

Jesper said nothing. He'd never forget his day in court, or his year in jail. All the showrooms had closed. The factory had closed. He'd defaulted on the loans. By the time he got out he was friendless and broke. But he hadn't thought about any of it for a while. Food was usually more pressing.

"Do you think it's fair that those same Swiss bankers got to keep their jobs and your money?" They both already knew the answer. But if Harg Heggle wanted a personalized homeless encounter, there wasn't much point in resisting. "Well?"

"No."

"What was that? I'm going to need you to enunciate, like when you sold me on dovetailed drawers."

"It was bullshit." He blinked, startled at his own voice.

Harg raised an eyebrow. "So you can still bite." His lip curled. "We'll clean you up, too," he added, more to himself than Jesper.

"Thank you," he said, relieved. He hadn't meant to speak so firmly. "Sir."

"You're welcome," Harg chuckled. "But wouldn't you like to know for what?"

"Okay." Jesper suppressed another cough. His feet were starting to hurt from standing.

Harg sighed. "Can you confirm that you're a legal citizen of Bermuda?"

"Left when I was four." Harg glared, prompting him to mumble, "Yes."

"Then you'll be moving back there." Harg looked over his shoulder and called, "Jacksbury."

A woman rose from a shadowed cluster of couches. She had short, dark hair and walked with perfect symmetry. She stopped beside the couch Harg was sitting on and stood with her hands still at her sides. Her face was almost expressionless. Almost. Jesper had learned to read faces over the past two years—who might drop a coin in his cup? Usually not the smiling ones. But she looked like she might have.

That evening Jesper stood at the entrance of Bethesda Heggle Spaceport. None of the other travelers looked twice. But now he couldn't stop looking at his own reflection in every glass door and bathroom mirror and polished surface he came across. He looked well. Clean-shaven, clean hair and skin and fingernails, leather shoes and fitted suit. He looked nothing like himself at any earlier time in his life, and that was fine.

Above the entrance's awning he could see a passenger shuttle rising atop a directed magnetic field. He heard a low thrumming, rising and ceasing, rising and ceasing. To the right, magnetic launchers shot unmanned freighters directly into lunar orbit.

Inside the ticketing agent scanned his eye and with no further questions sent him on to security. There a single guard scanned his eye again and pointed him toward a sparsely lit, bare concrete tunnel.

He'd never been off-planet before. Even at the peak of his furniture business, when he'd had enough money for tax havens to at least sound worthwhile, flying to the moon had seemed exorbitant, and pointless. He didn't really see the point of this trip, either—his final destination was Bermuda. "The moon is my base of operations," Harg had said. "This just simplifies the logistics." Jesper caught another glimpse of himself in a mirror in the tunnel. He resolved then that he would one, shave every day, and two, not question Harg's plans.

After what felt like miles, the tunnel opened into a hangar with forklifts moving between large metal containers, almost all of which had Jimenez Metals logos. Harg and Jesla were clearly more than acquaintances. There were a few people here, but they all wore yellow jumpsuits, and none paid Jesper more than a glance.

He was looking back at the tunnel when a woman said, "Jesper Torus."

It sounded like a summons. "Sorry." He tried to suppress a cough but failed. He stared at the ground, ready to be escorted out. At least the suit and shoes would look nice for another month.

"Look up, please," she said. He did, and she scanned his eye with a handheld reader. "Thank you. I'll escort you to your shuttle."

Your shuttle. So Harg had made special arrangements. "Thanks." It felt better than sorry.

Inside the shuttle faint red lights illuminated more metal containers. On the one nearest him he again saw the logo of Jimenez Metals.

"I've seen you before." The voice was too hoarse to say if it was male or female. "Gallery Place Chinatown."

The metro stop. Jesper had sat on a grate there when he'd begged during the last winter. The door slid shut behind him.

His companion cackled, coughed. "He gave me a fancy suit, too. But we can't hide the stench."

Jesper felt the shuttle lurch as it began to taxi. He sat down. "What is this?"

"Our second chance."

The shuttle stopped. Jesper heard the thrumming from earlier, deeper and louder and much closer. It grew until his eardrums ruptured. He realized he was in a freighter.

He lay down flat. He'd once contemplated jumping in front of a Greyhound. He imagined the moment of impact might have felt like the pressure on his back now. Fluid leaked from his ears and splattered wide across the floor. The last thing he felt were his ribs, a few at a time, bending and cracking into his lungs.

Jesper awoke to the sound of a seal pressurizing. The door slid open, and soft white light entered the freighter. He wasn't sure how much time had elapsed. His entire body—every part he could feel—was in pain, all-encompassing pain that drove everything else from his mind.

"Looks like one of them made it."

"Yes."

"What would Harg have done if they'd both made it?"

"Would you like to find out?"

"I wouldn't. No."

Jesper saw Jacksbury and a man in a yellow jumpsuit standing over him. They lifted—peeled—him up and into a medipod. On the floor below he could see his own blood, squished chunks of leg and torso, a flattened fingernail. Further inside the freighter he saw a mess of skin and blood and bones in what had probably been a fitted suit.

He heard Jacksbury say to the other, "Get a water jet," then lost consciousness.

"Wake up, Jesper." The voice was gravelly, but not coarse. Unrushed.

Jesper opened his eyes.

"Good morning, sleepyhead." A monitor displayed Harg sitting on one of his couches. He had his legs crossed and one arm stretched across the back. Jacksbury stood beside the monitor.

"You flew me to the moon to kill me." Which seemed convoluted. Surely trillionaires had other means, if perhaps not as painful. All he knew was that it had been intentional.

Three seconds later Harg said, "I require a certain level of obedience from my associates."

Jesper stared.

Harg smiled. "I just needed to make sure you wouldn't bite. I trust you're doing well now."

Jesper touched his chest. All ribs were in place. The rest of him looked to be in order, reconstituted, all fingernails accounted for. Through the window he saw the Earth, rising and huge on a gray horizon. A truck with large, bulbous wheels and a Jimenez Metals container on its bed bobbled past. "You killed the other." The realization dawned on him. "Everyone there killed him." Jesper had been obviously out of place. The ticketing and security agents, the people in the hangar—any one of them could have intervened.

"Don't forget it."

Harg continued to smile at Jesper. Jacksbury just stared. It was easy to imagine that she was disgusted, though her face revealed nothing. Standing there before them, Jesper felt more afraid than he'd thought himself capable of. In the last two years, he'd been punched in the face by a passing stranger, lost three teeth to an infection and woken up coughing on bloody pus each night, and eaten spoiled food too many times to count. He hadn't thought he could feel any more vulnerable than that.

But Harg was lord here. He was the playboy industrialist who'd brought the moon into the economy, but not into the law. Here he could have Jesper pushed into a vacuum. He could have him tortured, actually tortured, in front of all of his employees. No one would talk. He doubted anyone left the moon against Harg's wishes.

"What do you want from me?" Jesper said.

"Let me think about it." He touched a finger to his chin, as if deciding on an entrée. "How about a chair?"

"A chair?"

"Make me one."

Jacksbury led Jesper through a series of pristine white corridors. At each window, Jesper looked out at stars and blackness, and at his reflection. His body held no record of the agony on the freighter. Often during the last winter, when shivering in an unheated squat, or hungry, or outside with nowhere to urinate, he'd sometimes estimated the level of raw pain he'd endure for a reset. Apparently the freighter had been it.

They arrived at a domed room, about half the size of Harg's office. Near the wall were planks of wood of various sizes. In the center, circular saws and power sanders and a jointer-planer were arranged like a breakfast buffet. And there was a fridge and a sink, and a bathroom.

"You want me to start making furniture again?" He hoped he didn't sound too eager.

"Start with the chair," Jacksbury replied evenly.

"What style?"

"No frills."

No customer had ever said that to Jesper. Harg hadn't flipped a coin for his life so he could make Arts and Crafts style furniture on the moon. Jacksbury turned and, arms motionless at her sides, departed through the corridor.

"Wake up, Jesper." It was Harg again, on the monitor, smiling. He was in his office. An elephant tusk occupied the space above his head.

Jesper sat up. He'd slept on the floor. He rubbed his eyes as Jackbury walked in. Privacy was clearly not a priority.

"Let's have a look," Harg said.

Jesper stood up and walked over to the chair he'd made overnight. Or overday. He'd lost track on the freighter. He shrugged and placed a hand on the backrest.

"What am I looking at here? Sell it to me."

Jesper shifted his feet. "Quartersawn oak," he began.

Harg rolled his eyes. "I supplied the wood."

Jesper pointed under the seat. "Chi stretchers support the legs without limiting foot movement."

"Go on."

"Twenty-eight mortise and tenon joints." He felt a match-flame of confidence alight inside him. "Not a single nail."

"Even better."

"Modern backrest." He ran his fingers down a ladder of seven rails. Any more than three was unorthodox. "Obverse tapering seat." He paused, and then added, "I'm quite proud of it."

"I value honest work." The corners of Harg's eyes sharpened. "Pay him a fair price."

Jesper moved to stand behind the chair. His confidence melted as Jacksbury approached. 'Fair price' could mean a bullet or a knife. She frowned, faintly, but he could see the misery behind it, as if what she was about to do was worse than a simple execution. Jesper began to imagine a cycle of hope and pain, over and over until Harg got bored. The freighter had merely been the initiation.

Harg returned his attention to Jesper. "Deposit it as soon as you arrive."

Jacksbury pulled a slip of paper from her shirt pocket, handed it to Jesper, and left.

"And Jesper," Harg chuckled, "enjoy Bermuda!"

He didn't move after the monitor went black. Harg had to have better things to do than continue to observe him in secret, but he still felt watched. The hammer could strike at any moment. The freighter —the sudden, unexpected, crushing pressure—had imprinted a new kind of fear onto his mind.

After a minute he collapsed to a seat on the floor. He certainly wasn't going to sit in the chair. He was sure Harg had figured it out when he'd said 'obverse tapering seat.'

He really was proud of it. The seat was half an inch narrower in the front than back. The legs ended in pointed knobs that dug into the hamstrings. The 'modern backrest' was inclined eleven degrees from vertical—four more than the commonsense maximum of seven—and had no kicker. This chair was a dumper. And the armrests were too short. Inane, but in vogue—the perfect touch for the most spiteful chair Jesper had ever built. Whatever Harg believed, he could still bite.

He looked at the slip of paper Jacksbury had given him. It was a check. He sat for another hour, rereading it every few minutes.

It was for a trillion dollars.

Jesper stared out of the passenger shuttle's window. The wing glowed orange as the sky shifted from black to blue. He leaned back in his seat, wondering if Harg's couches were this comfortable.

"Another ginger ale?" asked the stewardess.

Jesper tested the can in front of him. "I haven't finished this one."

She smiled. "You can still have another."

"Okay." He quickly finished the can anyway. "Can I have another crème brûlée, too?"

"Of course, Mr. Torus." She placed a new can on his tray and walked up the aisle.

At a million a ticket, though complimentary for him, coach was certainly a step up from freight. And now he could take a million trips, if he wanted to. He hadn't taken the check out of his pocket since leaving the woodshop. He remembered once seeing an article about the world's first trillionaire, the founder of a company that mined cobalt for batteries. Harg was one, or had been until very recently, and now so was Jesper Torus.

The logic was clear enough. It would have been to anyone with his history. Bermuda had the lowest tax rate in the world: zero. Thanks to the International Open Banking Accord, the only way Harg could hide his fortune there was within someone else. Tax evasion, again. He didn't like it, but the chance to walk away had passed. He knew now that the alternative—going against Harg—would be far worse than jail.

"Here you go, Mr. Torus." The stewardess placed another crème brûlée on his tray.

"Thank you."

"Anything for a guest of Mr. Heggle."

Her smile lingered, and Jesper felt his pulse quicken. He supposed he was now Harg's banker. Or bank account. Objectively, he decided, it was an improvement.

Jacksbury picked up Jesper at Bermuda Heggle Spaceport and drove him directly to Bermuda International Bank in Hamilton. White showed where the building's yellow stucco had chipped. They entered through a cramped revolving door, and were greeted by a teller in boxy red polo shirt. He stood with several similarly uniformed employees behind a laminated particleboard counter.

Jesper glanced at Jacksbury. She inclined her head toward the counter. Jesper raised an eyebrow. He wasn't sure what he'd been expecting. Perhaps marble and brass and fountain pens, suits instead of polo shirts. Not what looked like a suburban branch in need of renovation. But Jacksbury smiled. It was the first smile he'd seen from her.

Jesper approached the teller. "I'd like to open an account."

"Your name, please?"

"Jesper Torus."

"Two forms of ID with proof of citizenship?"

Jesper placed his Bermudan birth certificate and expired Maryland driver's license on the counter.

The teller gave each half a glance and said, "Would you like to make an initial deposit?"

Jesper slid the check across on the counter.

The teller held it up between two fingers. For the past day Jesper had worried over creasing it while fighting the urge to look at it every few seconds, the whole time anticipating the present moment, on guard in case Harg had more surprises in store. The teller nodded, wrote something in a ledger, and placed it under the counter. Jesper let out an involuntary breath.

"Is there anything else I can help you with today?"

Jesper looked at his hands, still unused to how consistently clean they were. "That's all, I think."

"Then please enjoy the sunshine."

In the car Jesper kept the window down, watching the palm trees go by as Jacksbury drove. He smelled the ocean, heard waves on the beach. It was good to be home, he told himself, even a home he had no memory of. There'd be no need to claim subway grates here. Never again would he fold his hands between his legs and pretend his toes didn't exist. He could get a job to stay busy. Maybe he'd open a furniture shop. He had the money.

Harg's money, that was.

"You'll periodically be asked to buy things," Jacksbury said as they turned off the road onto a dirt path.

"By Harg."

"For Harg." She said nothing for a minute, and then added, "Don't get curious."

Jesper glanced at her. She somehow kept still over every bump and divot. She didn't seem at all perturbed. He wondered if he'd imagined what he'd heard in her voice: concern.

"Can I go out?" he asked.

"Within Bermuda." No inflection whatsoever.

"Can I buy things for myself?"

"Within reason."

"Can I work?"

"I don't see why not."

Was she amused or wistful? Perhaps she was also relieved about the check. She told him where to buy food, about the maid service and his wardrobe and how to access premium TV channels, and several other details of his new day-to-day existence.

The debriefing ended precisely as they pulled up to a house on the coast. Its walls were turquoise painted stone with red cedar storm shutters, and its white roof was stepped like a tiny ziggurat.

"The back has a nice view of the ocean."

Jesper smiled, and then realized that she was waiting for him to go. As he got out of the car, he saw a beach on the other side, too rocky for sunbathing but perfect for walking, and a veranda linking it to the house.

He shut the car door. Through the window Jacksbury said, "I'll check in periodically," and then drove off before he could reply.

Jesper watched the car vanish as the path wound into the trees. She certainly hadn't wanted to talk any longer than necessary, but she didn't seem to mind his company, either. He hadn't been anyone's company in years. He wondered just how periodically she was planning on checking in.

The next morning Jesper found a bicycle in the garage and rode it into Hamilton. He wasn't tired when he arrived downtown, and he still wasn't tired after another hour of searching. He was fit. He'd forgotten the rush that came with exercise. He almost let himself feel confident. Almost. He knew that he existed fully within Harg's dominion. What that meant, and the memory of the freighter, never left his thoughts.

He'd noticed other changes in his body in the shower the night before. Moles had gone missing, missing teeth had returned. His elbow didn't hurt when he soaped his back. It was as if he'd never had an injury or illness in his life. At the time he'd been too preoccupied with everything else to pay much notice, but now, pedaling and breathing, calmed by the ocean air, he began to wonder. Had Harg simply given him exhaustive repairs, or was there more?

The safety of Harg's money depended on Jesper's wellbeing, he reflected, and he hadn't been in great shape before. Harg had merely strengthened his asset.

Eventually he found a kitchen and bath store and locked up the bike out front. A woman slightly older than himself watched him enter.

He walked directly up to her, feeling healthy, focused, and said, "Do you do cabinetry?"

"Any hinge, door, or drawer you can think of."

"Tables, chairs, and beds?"

"Could, but don't."

"Then can you tell me where to find a sliding compound miter saw, a surface planer, and a quality supply of cedar?"

"Promise not to build any doors?"

"I promise."

"And no chests with more than three drawers?"

Jesper looked over the kitchen displays. The morning sun cast its shadows deep into the shop. He saw at least five different styles of sinks and stoves and cabinets, all modern, granite countertops and injection-molded knobs, no wood grain in sight.

"How about no metal drawer slides?" He half-smiled. This was the most he'd spoken in years. He certainly hadn't expected what he knew of negotiation to come back so easily. "Just guides. Wood on wood."

She shook his hand. He began to pull back, but she squeezed. All affability left her face. "No doors."

"I've no interest."

She released his hand and smiled. "Then you can find all the tools you need at McChuck's. Island Lumber has cedar, pine, and sapele. They'll give you wholesale prices if you tell them I sent you."

"And you are?"

"Donna."

"Thank you, Donna." He looked over the shop once more. None to his style, but it was all well done. "I'm Jesper."

As he turned to go she said, "No one else does Arts and Crafts on the island. I expect you'll do well."

"I'm just looking to keep busy."

She watched him at the door. He wondered if she still thought him a potential competitor. Her eyes flitted over his body, which had a light sheen of sweat from the bike ride. "There are other ways to keep busy," she said. Perhaps her interests weren't entirely professional. "For those who contribute to the island."

That evening, Jesper had dinner on the part of the veranda that faced the ocean. The sun was setting behind the house, and the tide made dusky islands of the rocks on the beach. It was all very pragmatic. The house was spacious, but not enough to make a single occupant feel isolated. No one would wander by, and he felt no urge to seek further comforts.

After dinner he pushed back his plate and reclined in his chair, listening to the water as the light faded. He heard a chime from his phone. It was an email from Harg.

The message read: 'Alpha Black Lotus. Bid 300K.' There was an eBay link.

It was some sort of collectible playing card. Jesper didn't see why Harg bothered with bidding instead of just buying it outright at a higher price. Then he recalled his furniture business. Footstool or four-poster bed, he'd never seen someone haggle for genuine financial reasons.

It wasn't important. Harg could buy what he wanted. He placed the bid, laid his phone on the table, and returned his attention to the night and the ocean.

Jesper stepped out of the shower, dried off, and dressed in the bathroom. He'd been living there four months and assumed there were cameras everywhere, except maybe the bathrooms. Even if they were monitored, it beat bathing in fountains and sneaking into basements of office buildings.

"You can replace more of the furniture," Jacksbury said as Jesper entered the kitchen. "If you want." She stood in the breakfast area, drinking beer from a can. She must have come in during his shower. At first he'd found the sight of her in any state of leisure odd, but within two or three check-ins she'd become a familiar, even calming presence. Since the second month he'd stocked pilsners just for her.

"I'm content with what you've provided." He'd fallen into the habit of addressing Jacksbury and Harg as one entity. Objectively, it wasn't rude. She was the one monitoring him, ensuring his participation in Harg's scheme, detaining him on the island. But he knew it was rude, because he wanted to see if it bothered her. "More than content."

In spite of the fact that he wasn't free, it was true. He might have once had more satisfaction—when he'd sold his first dining table, seen his showrooms full, floor models changing faster than he'd even hoped, and after hours in that same showroom proposed and made love. Back then, he was always looking forward.

But in the past four months he'd risen so far that he wanted only continuity—to go on building furniture, watching the ocean. Entertaining Jacksbury once or twice a week. No pain or torture, of course. It could happen again, yes, but it hadn't, and he saw no reason why it would.

Jacksbury said nothing and walked out to the veranda. She wasn't talkative, but had a slow to surface warmth—never an intimidating remark, never a reminder of the truth of his servitude. She'd seemed genuinely interested when she noticed the end table he'd put beside the couch. He didn't mind that her interest was probably part of Harg's program to keep him docile. Perhaps Jacksbury also liked things the way they were. He knew so little about her, and he dared not ask.

The purchases, on the other hand, were almost dull in their random extravagance. He didn't see why Jacksbury had felt the need to warn him. There were more collectible cards, sculptures and paintings, old books. He could understand how someone like Harg would struggle to find satisfaction. A 1901 Stickley armchair, a townhouse in San Francisco, a professional hockey team. Legally, Jesper now owned these things. Some he wished he actually did. Persian rugs, an espresso machine, intellectual property. He wondered how much time a day Harg spent shopping.

That evening he dined with Jacksbury on the veranda. They sat at a pine dining table Jesper had built, slatted for when it rained, and ate lentil soup with a baguette he'd baked earlier that day.

"How is it?" he asked.

"Could use more salt."

"The bread or the soup?"

"Both."

"I could add celeriac to the soup." Jesper thought for a second. "It's hard to find here. Do you mind if I order some from off the island?" Which was to say, did Harg mind?

"I doubt it."

She couldn't have sounded less bothered than that. Of course Harg didn't mind, and as far as he knew, she didn't seem to mind Harg.

"I'll go ahead then."

He often found himself waiting for her to say more. Each night she was over, there'd come a point where she'd focus on the water and tighten her lips, seemingly in concentration, looking for the right words. Then she'd exhale, smile briefly, and say nothing. Maybe it was hard to find a version she could say under Harg's eye. Or, maybe it was an act to keep him from getting too bored. Either way, he'd decided, the company was nice. He was happy to go on waiting.

Later that night, after she'd retired to the guest quarters, his phone chimed. 'Cloudlight Mach 13.' Harg had mentioned in an early email that Cloudlight Mach was a family of patents. Apparently he liked to own them personally. Jesper purchased it directly from the seller and laid the phone back on the table. The night was clear. He could see the ocean miles out, where moonlight slid like oil over low and distant waves. His phone chimed again. 'Cloudlight Mach 9,' and before he'd put it down, 'Cloudlight Mach 20.'

Harg had never before requested more than one purchase in a night. Cloudlight sounded technological, aerospacey, although Mach number made no sense in a vacuum. Maybe it had to do with takeoff from earth, or reentry. He made the purchases and laid his phone on the table, slightly annoyed. He knew he had no right to be annoyed. He wasn't sure he had any rights in matters not aligned with Harg's will. But it was hard to settle into ocean gazing when always expecting another chime. There was room for basic courtesy.

He searched online for 'Cloudlight Mach,' curious what new technology could be so urgent. The search results had just finished loading on his phone when the waves began to glow, ripples of moonlight pulsing so intensely that his vision blurred. His shoulder throbbed. He vomited on himself and the table. He couldn't breathe. The waves were painfully bright, and then all was dark. He couldn't move his legs enough to push back his chair, and his voice made no sound when he tried to call for Jacksbury.

"Wake up, Jesper."

He opened his eyes. He was in his bed in the master bedroom. His head hurt, but his body felt okay. Harg smiled. Jesper thought he was there in person until he noticed the taxidermied elephant ear behind him. He realized that he was seeing Harg on a monitor he'd thought was a simple mirror. Jacksbury stood next to the monitor, motionless, expressionless.

Jesper remembered feeling sick and passing out. He remembered the first search result. "You made me buy rhino horns on the black market." Cloudlight Mach was just the code name.

"Abhorrent, I know. There are so few black rhinos left. But I need to convince someone to let me build a spaceport in

Calgary, and I just can't think of a better gift."

"I never agreed to that."

Harg chuckled. "I'd assumed you had the sense not to pry. You never bothered before. But apparently you're just incurious."

Jesper wondered how much Jacksbury had known. She'd warned him earlier for a reason. It didn't matter. "Never again."

"I tried sitting in the chair you made me," Harg said as he rose from one of his couches. "It wasn't very comfortable. It made me wonder if it was an honest effort. Perhaps another ride on a freighter is in order." Jesper resisted the urge to flinch, but Harg clearly noticed. He grinned. The levity was gone from his eyes, the creases more decrepit than gentle. "You had quite the heart attack last night. Natural causes, of course. Good thing you already have a will."

So that was the full extent of Harg's repairs to Jesper's body: remote-controlled termination. Harg was obviously the will's sole beneficiary. Jacksbury would know if Jesper made a new one, not that it would have made much difference. None of this was his, not the house or the food or the tools in his new workshop. He owned nothing because Harg owned him. He might as well have died on the freighter, or jumped in front of a Greyhound, or frozen on the sidewalk—all of which were worse ways to go than a heart attack. "So kill me."

Jesper could see Harg's jaw working beneath his smile. He heard a faint scratch. Beside the monitor, Jacksbury stood like a statue.

"I think you know that I'd rather not," Harg replied. "For logistical reasons. But I'm willing to go through as many replacements as necessary."

Jesper felt his stomach turn. He'd be sick, but not like last night. Harg would have his purchases. At best, Jesper could inflict some inconvenience, and at the cost of his life. And perhaps it was worth it.

He clenched his fists, breathed slowly. He remembered the many hours in his old workshop, his fiancée before the trial, the moment of the verdict. He'd felt relieved, unburdened at the time. It was the last he ever saw of his would be wife. He gazed at Jacksbury. She was a better last sight than he might have hoped for. He parted his lips to speak.

There was a soft tap, almost lost in the wind and waves. Jacksbury stood still save one finger, touching the wall and then returning to symmetry.

Harg took his phone out of his pocket and looked up at Jesper. "Well?" His finger hovered over the screen.

Jesper glanced again at Jacksbury. Nothing. But there had been something. He'd never know what it was if he died. "I would like to live."

The gentleness returned to Harg's eyes, though a question lingered.

"Please."

"The next one is a ploughshare tortoise shell. To go on my coffee table." Harg put away his phone, and the monitor was once again a mirror.

Jacksbury left without a word. Jesper sat on the bed. A few minutes later his phone chimed. 'Cloudlight Mach 23.' There could be one alive in the world for all he knew. He made the purchase, tossed the phone on the bed, and went to the bathroom to vomit.

Later that day, Jesper stood on the beach barefoot. It was January, and the ocean was cold. Not like winter in the city, but not pleasant. Erratic gusts of wind snapped the palm leaves. The sun shone bright over the ocean but provided no warmth. He squinted by reflex, ignoring the chill accumulating in his feet. He couldn't stand to be in the house or the veranda or the workshop, where Harg might watch him at any time. Everything was tainted.

He had to find out what Jacksbury had to say. A scratch and a tap. He couldn't think of a less significant pair of gestures. But nothing was accidental with Jacksbury. Maybe it was a feint, a distraction with no purpose other than to further his servitude. If so it wouldn't work. He'd just refuse to make Harg's next purchase and be done with it.

His feet were starting to hurt. Like walking through snow in torn sweatpants and sneakers he'd worn every day for a year. He felt himself becoming obsessed with Jacksbury. Either she wanted to help him or Jesper was going to die. She certainly couldn't say it in the house.

He decided to go out on the bike, thinking exercise might help him see things more clearly. The bike leaned against a sawhorse in the garage-turned-workshop. He surveyed his tools and some unfinished tables and chairs, all sullied by his true purpose here. Harg wasn't a sadist. He just liked evil things, and sometimes used sadism to obtain them.

He rode out onto the dirt path. He was dressed too lightly, and the cool air made his joints feel stiff. There was little point in worrying over comforts now. He stopped suddenly where the path turned to meet the road.

An old sail hung between two trees, flapping in the wind. It hadn't been there the last time he'd gone out. 'Donna's Kitchen and Bath' had been hastily painted over mildew stains. He pulled down the sail, tossed it into the trees, and took off toward Hamilton.

His clothes were matted with cold sweat by the time he reached the store. He left the bike lying on the sidewalk. The wind had made his eyes water, leaving dried streaks on his cheeks. Donna watched him enter with the same skepticism as before.

"I've come to regret our deal," she said.

Jesper stared as he caught his breath.

"No one wants drawers with metal slides anymore," she went on. "Just wood on wood from you."

The compliment felt perverse against the revelations of the past twenty-four hours. "What do you want?"

Jacksbury stepped out from behind an oven and sink display.

"Something I'm sure you'll agree to," Donna said flatly.

That evening Jesper sat on the veranda watching the ocean. He wore a wool sweater and a pair of slacks he'd found in the master bedroom. He finished his dinner, refilled his wine glass, and waited. The leaves on the palm trees fluttered in the wind. Waves hewed into each other before reaching the shore, their whitecaps colliding in bursts of foam.

His phone chimed. 'Cloudlight Mach 41.'

He looked at Jacksbury. She nodded once and returned her gaze to the ocean. Jesper wrote back 'Sorry, insufficient funds.'

If Harg was feeling levelheaded, he had a chance. If impulsive, a fatal heart attack was moments away. Both moods struck Jesper as fundamental to a spaceflight tycoon. Jacksbury remained silent and still, save the slow nodding motion of her foot. She was nervous.

A moment later Harg appeared. The table cut him off at his waist. "Ten seconds to explain," said the hologram.

"There isn't enough money left."

Harg took a phone out of his shirt pocket. Through the hologram Jesper could see the ocean churning.

"It's not gone," Jesper added quickly. "I just don't have it."

Harg smiled through gritted teeth. "Then who does?"

"I do," said Donna as she entered the veranda from the beach. She left a trail of wet footprints on the floorboards.

"And why do you have my money?"

"I believe the money was Jesper's before it became mine," Donna replied. A scowl slipped through Harg's grin. "I sold him some cabinets for around a trillion dollars."

Jesper said, "I've done Arts and Crafts my whole life. I was in the mood for something more modern. I sold her a very traditional Mission Style end table, by the way."

"Also for around a trillion dollars, I suppose," Harg said, the rasp in his voice rising to a growl.

"That's correct," Jesper replied.

"So you traded money." Harg extended a finger over his phone. "I'll inherit a trillion regardless."

Jesper gripped his chair in a moment of panic. His heart began to pound. Did he feel nauseous? There was a script, but no guarantee Harg would follow it. Perhaps there was a delay in the signal, and Harg had already murdered him.

"Minus a trillion," Donna said. "We signed new wills at Bermuda International Bank this afternoon. Any money I paid to Jesper goes back to me if he dies, and vice versa."

Harg withdrew his finger. The hologram sank a foot into the table as Harg sat on one of his couches. Jesper let out a trembling breath. He wasn't dead yet. If Harg killed him, Donna would inherit everything in his account. If Donna died, Jesper would inherit a trillion from her.

"Then I suppose I'll have to kill you both—starting with you, so Jesper can first receive his inheritance," he said as he settled onto the couch. "Jacksbury."

"Go ahead," Donna said. Harg raised an eyebrow. "Although then you might upset Jesla Jimenez."

Harg held up a hand, unaware that Jacksbury hadn't moved. "And why would Jesla Jimenez care?"

"A couple years ago I sold her a kitchen island for two trillion dollars," Donna answered. "You can guess why. I believe Jimenez Metals is the primary importer of moon ore. Jesla doesn't appreciate… inconveniences. Or am I confusing her with someone else?"

Harg crossed his legs and chuckled to himself. He was trying to project calm, control. Jesper would have bought it, too, were the hologram not of such high quality. A cheaper system wouldn't have showed the gritted teeth behind his smile, how firmly his fingers were dug into his couch, the depth of the wrinkles around his eyes, like cracks in marble. "I think a quick conversation with Jesla might clear up this…mess," he said, almost snarling.

"Doubtful." Donna shook her head at the floor. "I've done kitchen and bath work for quite a few of us…offshores." She gestured to herself and Jesper.

"We're all tangled up here on the island," Jesper said. "My codicil actually specifies seventeen beneficiaries in addition to Donna, and each of them has their own set. You'd have to kill a few dozen of us to get everything back. I don't think even you could manage that."

"Screw Jesla Jimenez." Harg threw his phone out of the hologram. "I'll at least get some of my money back if I kill the two of you. Draw it out, Jacksbury." He waited, quivering with suppressed rage. "Jacksbury!"

Jacksbury didn't move from her seat. She glared at the hologram. "I'm not proud of a single thing I've done for you."

"Jacksbury," he seethed.

"My name is Jacqueline."

Harg looked as if he would have gone for Jesper's throat had he been physically present. "If my money is gone no matter what, tell me why I shouldn't kill you right now," he shouted, "you useless bum!"

Jesper remained seated. He wanted to shout back, to tell Harg how little he thought of him, that he'd seen how petty and selfish he really was. But Harg could pick up his phone and kill him at any moment. If he got any angrier, he probably would. Jesper kept his expression neutral, his voice flat. He hoped his heartbeats weren't audible. "Because I will give you an allowance of one billion dollars a week. I don't want your money, but I need leverage. You'll have almost of it back in twenty years."

It was hard to imagine Harg surrendering, but he didn't argue. He just glared. Jesper could almost feel his temperature rising. "Almost?"

"Minus the taxes I've helped you avoid, and minus one billion for each dead animal I've helped you buy. Those will go toward the establishment of the Harg Heggle Wildlife Fund." Jesper couldn't stop him. He didn't see how anyone really could. But he hoped the attention would be enough to deter Harg Heggle, nature's newest defender, from making any further acquisitions.

Harg said nothing. His breathing returned to normal, and his face regained its usual calm. He smiled, and soft, gentle wrinkles spread out from each eye, each rendered in perfect holographic detail. Jesper suddenly regretted addressing him so boldly. He'd been level but firm when he should have begged. He felt certain that Harg had intuited a way to recover his money and kill him outright. Death would come without notice or explanation, and perhaps for Donna and Jacksbury—Jacqueline—as well. He should have known better.

Harg smiled. At the end of a full minute he said, "Sure," and the hologram blinked off.

They sat in silence for several seconds. Jesper felt deflated. Harg seemed to have acquiesced, but his tone had said otherwise. "I'm so sorry," Jesper said as his eyes adjusted. He could see stars and the swaying silhouettes of palm trees. Waves crashed in the veranda's glow, like wolves feinting toward a campfire. "It seems we failed."

Jacqueline made a faint snort, just less than a scoff. Jesper turned to face her. Loyalty—unflinching and to Harg and Harg only—had to be the primary requirement of her job. He didn't even feel betrayed, just stupid.

"You're not going to die," she said.

"Are you sure?" Donna asked. "Harg seemed pretty comfortable just now."

"That's his favorite tactic when he's run out of ways to get what he wants—act pleased, sow doubt. It usually brings his opponents back to the table. I never really got why it was so effective until now."

"Then we're going to be fine?" Donna said.

"So it would seem."

They waited for her to continue, but she only drew in a breath, tightened her lips, and stared out at the ocean. Jesper smiled to himself. It was like any of their nights together, except that they no longer cared if Harg was watching.

Donna unfolded her arms, said, "Looks like you two could use some time alone," and walked into the house.

Jacqueline continued to stare, her face neutral, though Jesper thought he'd seen her blush at Donna's exit. At the sound of the front door closing she turned. "I'm so sorry, Jesper."

If she had blushed before, it wasn't out of coyness. Misery, shame, fear—all were on her face. The only apologies Jesper had received in the past two years were from smiling people with no money or food to give him. He hadn't expected to hear one now. "Are you still working for Harg?" He could hear the fear in his voice. He'd never stopped expecting a reckoning, he realized, when the springs would release and the trap would fling him further down than ever before. A final heart attack, another ride on a freighter, delivered by the only person he'd felt any attachment to in years.

"No." She tried to smile, but it didn't stick. "Never again."

Jesper nodded, relieved, but before he could speak she said, "I'm sorry for keeping you here these past four months. And I'm sorry about the freighter. When I saw you in there…maimed…I didn't know what Harg was planning, but I could have guessed that it was something terrible. I should have defied him, like you did. Years ago."

She stood up and started into the house.

"Jacks—Jacqueline," Jesper said, panicking.

She stopped. Jesper could see how tense she was, in the spread of her fingers, the odd angle of her arms. It was as if she'd forgotten how to stand. She angled her head to listen without eye contact. "Harg wanted me to sound like a butler," she said.

"I forgive you."

She turned to face him. "Just like that?"

"Yes." More than yes. The memory of the freighter still hurt. It hurt Jacqueline, too. They'd both get over it with Harg gone. He hoped that the last four months hadn't been all suffering for her because, in spite of the circumstances, he'd found the last four months wonderful. "Where will you go?"

She shrugged. She had nothing outside of Harg's empire. Nor did he, except for a local furniture business and a very substantial bank account.

"Why don't you stay here?"

"I'm surprised you can stand me."

"Of course I can stand you." As coolly as he could manage, he said, "I like you." He didn't want to sound too interested. But not disinterested, either. One essential modification presented itself. "I think I'll buy a new house. One without any cameras in it."

She let out a nervous laugh, walked back to her chair, and sat down. "I saw a place in Hog Bay yesterday. Three beds, three baths, new kitchen. Unfurnished." Jesper nodded, smiling. "No hidden retinal scanners, palm or fingerprint readers, or microphones. And no optical topographers in the showers or pressure sensors under the floors."

Jesper stiffened. He lifted his feet, grinned, and put them gently back on the wood. "That's good."

"And no wireless transmitter for the hundreds of nanochips Harg had implanted in your body."

"This house is on sale now?"

"The realtor said I could view it tonight. Would you like to come with me?"

See Josh Taylor's story "The Offshore" online at Metaphorosis.
If you liked it, leave a comment. Authors love that!
Remember to subscribe to our e-mail updates so you'll know when new stories are posted.

About the story

I recently read the book *The Hidden Wealth of Nations: The Scourge of Tax Havens* by Gabriel Zucman, which I recommend to anyone interested in the topic. People evade taxes by putting their money in other countries with lower tax rates. Anonymous bank accounts and shell companies make it possible to do it in a way that looks legal.

So what if anonymous bank accounts and shell companies were no longer an option? I suppose that would reduce tax evasion. But tax evasion strikes me as something with whack-a-mole qualities—get rid of one form and another pops up. For example, a person living in a place with low taxes could store someone else's money in their own bank account. And if someone who was wealthy and powerful wanted to store their money this way, in a person, they'd probably take some steps to ensure that person's cooperation.

That was the starting point. I thought it would lead to a relatively short short story. But other elements found their way in, particularly the year of research I did before buying my first non-IKEA dresser, and some longing for warmer weather, and it turned into the longest story I've written.

A question for the author

Q: What other writers inspire you?

A: This is a hard question to answer concisely! There are many writers I enjoy, and many writers that inspire me in writing and other ways. So I'll pick two that I don't think are mainstream now in speculative fiction.

I like reading about infrastructure, and my favorite such book is *The Big Necessity* by Rose George—unfashionable topic, new stuff in every chapter instead of variations of one main idea, a real balance of skepticism and optimism, and humor that's funny but respectful. And unlike most nonfiction books, I can still remember some of what it was about.

In fiction, I recently read *Seize the Day* and *Herzog* by Saul Bellow. I always assumed that he'd be too hard to read to enjoy, when in fact he's right on the line. It's an effort, for me, and not a lot happens, but he is so funny. Herzog brought the phrase 'ludicrous shmegeggy' into American literature. I didn't know it was possible to take apart a characters to such a degree, and without ever dropping long, twisty sentences that take multiple readings just to parse.

About the author

Josh Taylor was born in Baltimore and lives in Toronto. In addition to science fiction, he enjoys playing squash and baking cakes, but lately has only had time for cakes.

joshbtaylor.home.blog

Copyright

Metaphorosis Publishing

Metaphorosis offers beautifully written science fiction and fantasy. Our projects include:

Metaphorosis Magazine

Metaphorosis, a weekly magazine of SFF short stories, including stories from all the authors in this anthology. Find out more at magazine.metaphorosis.com, and sign up to be notified of new stories.

Metaphorosis Books

Recent books from Metaphorosis can be found at books.metaphorosis.com, and include:

Score

an SFF symphony

What if stories were written like music? *Score* is an anthology of stories written to an emotional score.

Best Vegan SFF of 2018

The best vegan science fiction and fantasy stories of 2018!

Metaphorosis 2018	**Metaphorosis: Best of 2018**
All the stories from *Metaphorosis* magazine's third year. Fifty-two great SFF stories.	The best science fiction and fantasy stories from *Metaphorosis* magazine's third year.

Metaphorosis
2017

All the stories from *Metaphorosis* magazine's second year. Fifty-three great SFF stories.

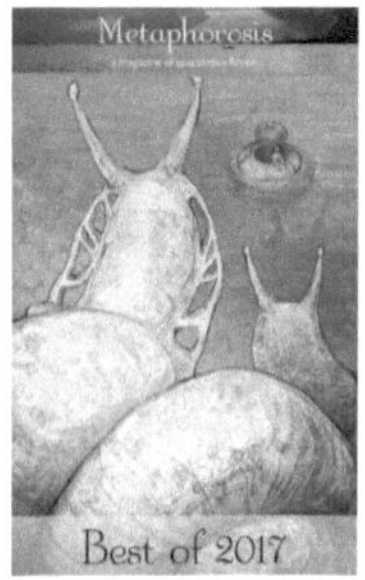

Metaphorosis:
Best of 2017

The best science fiction and fantasy stories from *Metaphorosis* magazine's *second* year.

Metaphorosis
2016

Almost all the stories from *Metaphorosis* magazine's first year.

Metaphorosis:
Best of 2016

The best science fiction and fantasy stories from *Metaphorosis* magazine's first year.

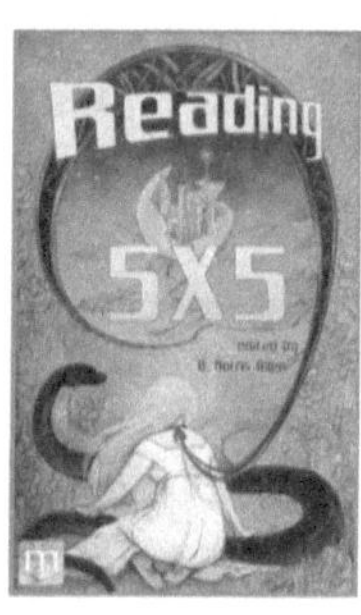 

Reading 5X5	**Reading 5X5**

Five stories, five times

Twenty-five SFF authors, five base stories, five versions of each – see how different writers take on the same material, with stories in contemporary and high fantasy, soft and hard SF, and a mysterious 'other' category.

Writers' Edition

All the stories from the regular, readers' edition, plus two extra stories, the story seed, and authors' notes on writing. Over 100 pages of additional material specifically aimed at writers.

Best Vegan SFF of 2017

Best Vegan SFF of 2016

The best vegan science fiction and fantasy stories of 2017!

The best vegan science fiction and fantasy stories of 2016!

Susurrus

A darkly romantic story of magic, love, and suffering.

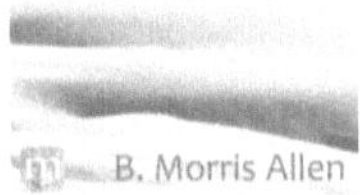

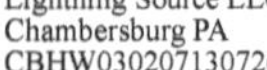